Pinocchio

Carlo Collodi

First published in 2021 by Miles Kelly Publishing Ltd
Harding's Barn, Bardfield End Green, Thaxted, Essex, CM6 3PX, UK

Copyright © Miles Kelly Publishing Ltd 2021

2 4 6 8 10 9 7 5 3

Publishing Director Belinda Gallagher
Creative Director Jo Cowan
Editorial Director Rosie Neave
Senior Editor Fran Bromage
Design Manager Joe Jones
Cover Designer Jo Cowan
Image Manager Liberty Newton
Production Controller Jennifer Brunwin
Reprographics Stephan Davis
Assets Lorraine King

Cover illustration Ciara Ni Dhuinn,
Plum Pudding Illustration Agency

The publisher would like to thank Vic Parker
for her help in compiling this book.

ISBN 978-1-78989-185-0

Printed in China

British Library Cataloguing-in-Publication Data
A catalogue record for this book is available from the British Library

Made with paper from a sustainable forest

www.mileskelly.net

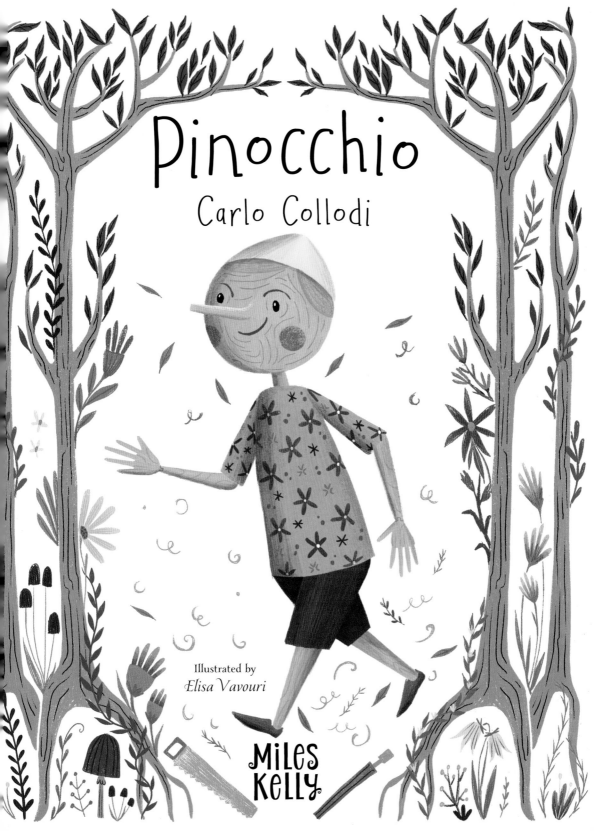

Pinocchio

Carlo Collodi

Illustrated by
Elisa Vavouri

MiLES KELLY

Contents

Chapter 1

How it came to pass that Master Cherry, the carpenter,
found a piece of wood that laughed and cried like a child.

THERE was once upon a time...

"A king!" my little readers will instantly exclaim.

No, children, you are wrong. There was, once upon a time, a piece of wood.

This wood was not valuable; it was only a common log like those that are burnt in winter in the stoves and fireplaces to make a cheerful blaze and warm the rooms.

I cannot say how it came about, but the fact is that one fine day this piece of wood was lying in the shop of an old carpenter of the name of Master Antonio. He was, however, called by everybody Master Cherry, on account of the end of his nose, which was always as red and polished as a ripe cherry.

No sooner had Master Cherry set eyes on the piece of wood than his face beamed with delight and, rubbing his hands together with satisfaction, he said softly to himself: "This wood has come at the right moment; it will just do to make the leg of a little table."

Having said this, he immediately took a sharp axe with which to remove the bark and the rough surface. Just, however, as he was going to give the first stroke he remained with his arm suspended in the air, for he heard a very small voice saying imploringly, "Do not strike me so hard!"

Imagine the astonishment of good old Master Cherry!

Chapter 1

He turned his terrified eyes all round the room to try and discover where the little voice could possibly have come from, but he saw nobody! He looked under the bench – nobody; he looked into a cupboard that was always shut – nobody; he looked into a basket of shavings and sawdust – nobody; he even opened the door of the shop and gave a glance into the street – and still nobody. Who, then, could it be?

"I see how it is," he said, laughing and scratching his wig, "evidently that little voice was all my imagination. Let us set to work again." And taking up the axe he struck a tremendous blow on the piece of wood.

"Oh! Oh! You have hurt me!" cried the same little voice, dolefully.

This time Master Cherry was petrified. His eyes started out of his head with fright, his mouth gaped open, and his tongue hung out almost to the end of his chin. As soon as he had recovered the use of his speech, he began to say, stuttering and trembling with fear: "But where on earth can that little voice have come from that said 'Oh! Oh!'…? There is certainly not a living soul here. Is it possible that this piece of wood can have learnt to cry and to wail like a child? I cannot believe it. This piece of wood – here it is – a log for fuel like all the others, and thrown on the fire it would about suffice to boil a saucepan of beans… How then? Can anyone be hidden inside it? If anyone is hidden inside, so much the worse for him. I will settle him at once."

So saying, he seized the poor piece of wood and began beating it without mercy against the walls of the room.

Finally he stopped to listen, to see if he could hear any little voice wailing. He waited two minutes – nothing; five minutes – nothing; ten minutes – still nothing!

"I see how it is," he then said, forcing himself to laugh and pushing up his wig, "evidently the little voice that said 'Oh! Oh!' was all my imagination! Let me set to work again."

Pinocchio

As all the same he was in a great fright, he tried to sing to give himself a little courage. Putting the axe aside, he took his plane, to plane and polish the bit of wood. But whilst he was running it up and down, he heard the same little voice say, laughing, "Have done! You are tickling me all over!"

This time poor Master Cherry fell down as if he had been struck by lightning. When he at last opened his eyes he found himself seated on the floor. His face was quite changed; the end of his nose, instead of being crimson as it nearly always was, had become blue from fright.

Chapter 2

Master Cherry makes a present of the piece of wood to his friend Geppetto, who takes it to make for himself a wonderful puppet, that knows how to dance and fence, and leap like an acrobat.

A<small>T</small> that moment someone knocked at the door.

"Come in," said the carpenter, without having the strength to rise to his feet.

A lively little old man immediately walked into the shop. His name was Geppetto, but when the boys of the neighbourhood wished to annoy him they called him by the nickname of Polendina, the name of the Italian corn pudding, because that is what his yellow wig looked just like.

Geppetto was very fiery. Woe to him who called him Polendina! He became furious and there was no holding him.

"Good day, Master Antonio," said Geppetto. "What are you doing there on the floor?"

"I am teaching the alphabet to the ants."

"Much good may that do you."

"What has brought you to me, neighbour Geppetto?"

"My legs. But to say the truth, Master Antonio, I have come to ask a favour of you."

"Here I am, ready to serve you," replied the carpenter, getting on to his knees.

"This morning an idea came into my head. I thought I would make a beautiful wooden puppet; but a wonderful puppet that knows how to dance, to fence, and to leap like an acrobat. With this puppet I would travel about the world to earn a piece of bread and a glass of wine. What do you think?"

"Bravo, Polendina!" exclaimed the same little voice – and it was impossible to say where it came from.

Hearing himself called Polendina, Geppetto became as red as a turkey-cock from rage and, turning to the carpenter, he said in a fury: "Why do you insult me?"

"Who insults you?"

"You called me Polendina!"

"It was not I!"

"Would you have it, then, that it was I? It was you, I say!"

"No!"

"Yes!"

"No!"

"Yes!"

And becoming more and more angry, from words they came to blows. Flying at each other, they bit and fought and scratched manfully.

When the fight was over, Master Antonio was in possession of Geppetto's yellow wig, and Geppetto discovered that the grey wig belonging to the carpenter was between his teeth.

"Give me back my wig," screamed Master Antonio.

"And you return me mine and let us make friends."

The two old men, having each recovered his own wig, shook hands and swore that they would remain friends to the end of their lives.

"Well then, neighbour Geppetto," said the carpenter, to prove that peace was made, "what is the favour that you wish of me?"

"I want a little wood to make my puppet; will you give me some?"

Master Antonio was delighted, and he immediately went to the bench and fetched the piece of wood that had caused him so much

fear. But, just as he was going to give it to his friend, the piece of wood gave a shake. Wriggling violently out of his hands, it struck with all its force against the dried-up shins of poor Geppetto.

"Ow! Is that the way in which you give your presents, Master Antonio? You have almost lamed me!"

"I swear to you that it was not me!"

"Then you would have it that it was me?"

"The wood is entirely to blame!"

"I know it was the wood; but it was you that hit my legs with it!"

"I did not hit you with it!"

"Liar!"

"Geppetto, don't insult me or I will call you Polendina!"

"Donkey!"

"Polendina!"

On hearing himself called Polendina again, Geppetto, blind with rage, fell upon the carpenter and they fought desperately.

When the battle was over, Master Antonio had two more scratches on his nose and his adversary had two buttons too few on his waistcoat. Their accounts being thus squared, they shook hands and swore to remain good friends for the rest of their lives.

Geppetto carried off his fine piece of wood and, thanking Master Antonio, returned limping to his house.

Chapter 3

Geppetto, having returned home, begins at once to make a puppet, to which he gives the name of Pinocchio. The puppet plays his first tricks...

Geppetto lived in a small ground-floor room that was only lit from the staircase. The furniture could not have been simpler: a bad chair, a poor bed, and a broken-down table. At the end of the room there was a fireplace with a lit fire – but the fire was painted, and by the fire was a painted saucepan that was boiling cheerfully and sending out a cloud of smoke that looked exactly like real smoke.

As soon as he reached home, Geppetto took his tools and set to work to cut out and model his puppet.

"What name shall I give him?" he said to himself. "I think I will call him Pinocchio. It is a name that will bring him luck. I once knew a whole family so called. There was Pinocchio the father, Pinocchia the mother, and Pinocchi the children – and all of them did well. The richest of them was a beggar."

Having found a name for his puppet he began to work in good earnest. First he made his hair, then his forehead, and then his eyes.

When the eyes were finished, imagine Geppetto's astonishment when he saw that they moved and looked fixedly at him!

Geppetto was very taken aback and said angrily: "Wicked wooden eyes, why do you look at me?"

No one answered.

He then proceeded to carve the nose... but no sooner had he made it than it began to grow. And it grew, and grew, and grew, until in a few minutes it had become an immense nose that seemed as if it would never end.

Poor Geppetto tired himself out with cutting it off; but the more he cut and shortened it, the longer did that impertinent nose become!

The mouth was not even completed when it began to laugh and deride him.

"Stop laughing!" said Geppetto, provoked.

The mouth then ceased laughing, but put out its tongue as far as it would go.

Geppetto, not to spoil his handiwork, pretended not to see and continued his labours. After the mouth he fashioned the chin, then the throat, then the shoulders, the stomach, the arms and the hands.

The hands were scarcely finished when Geppetto felt his wig snatched from his head. He turned round and what did he see? He saw his yellow wig in the puppet's hand.

"Pinocchio! Give me back my wig instantly!"

But Pinocchio, instead of returning it, put it on his own head – and was as a result nearly smothered by it.

Geppetto felt more melancholy than he had ever been before. Turning to Pinocchio, he said: "You young rascal! You are not yet completed and you are already beginning to show lack of respect to your father! That is bad, my boy, very bad!" And he dried a tear.

When Geppetto had finished the legs and feet, he received a kick on the point of his nose.

"I should have seen that coming!" he said to himself.

He then took the puppet under the arms and placed him on the floor to teach him to walk. Pinocchio's legs were stiff and he could not move, but Geppetto led him by the hand and showed him how to put one foot before the other.

When his legs became flexible, Pinocchio began to walk by himself

and to run about the room; until, having gone out of the house door, he jumped into the street and escaped.

Poor Geppetto rushed after him but was not able to overtake him, for that rascal Pinocchio leapt in front of him like a hare and, knocking his wooden feet together against the pavement, made as much clatter as twenty pairs of peasants' clogs.

"Stop him! Stop him!" shouted Geppetto. But the people in the street, seeing a wooden puppet running like a racehorse, stood still in astonishment to look at it and laughed.

At last, as good luck would have it, a cavalry soldier arrived who planted himself courageously with his legs apart in the middle of the road, barricading it.

Pinocchio tried to take the soldier by surprise and squeeze through his legs, but he failed dismally. The soldier caught him cleverly by his immense nose and delivered him to Geppetto.

Wishing to punish Pinocchio, Geppetto intended to pull his ears at once. But he had forgotten to make them! He then took Pinocchio by the collar and led him away, saying threateningly: "As soon as we arrive home, we'll settle this, don't doubt it."

At this, Pinocchio threw himself on the ground and would not take another step. A crowd of idlers and curious passers-by assembled in a ring round them.

"Poor puppet!" said several. "He is right not to wish to return home! Geppetto will beat him!"

Others added maliciously: "Geppetto is quite capable of tearing him in pieces!"

It ended in so much being said and done that the soldier at last set Pinocchio free and marched Geppetto off to prison.

What happened afterwards is a story that really is past all belief. But I will relate it to you in the following chapters...

Chapter 4

The story of Pinocchio and the Talking Cricket, from which we see that naughty boys cannot stand to be corrected by those who know more than they do.

WELL then, children, I must tell you that whilst poor Geppetto was being taken to prison for no fault of his, that imp Pinocchio ran off as fast as his legs could carry him.

Arriving home, he went in, secured the door, seated himself on the ground and gave a great sigh of satisfaction.

But his satisfaction did not last long, for he heard someone in the room who was saying: "Cri-cri-cri!"

"Who is calling me?" said Pinocchio in a fright.

"It is I!"

Pinocchio turned round and saw a big cricket crawling slowly up the wall.

"Tell me, Cricket, who may you be?"

"I am the Talking Cricket, and I have lived in this room a hundred years and more."

"However, this room is now mine," said the puppet, "and if you would do me a favour, go away at once without even turning round."

"I will not go," answered the Cricket, "until I have told you a truth."

"Tell it me, then – and be quick about it."

"Woe to those boys who rebel against their parents and run away capriciously from home. They will never come to any good in the world and, sooner or later, they will repent bitterly."

Pinocchio

"Sing away, Cricket, for as long as you please. For I have made up my mind to run away tomorrow at daybreak. If I remain I shall not escape the fate of all other boys: I shall be sent to school and made to study. And to tell you in confidence, I have no wish to learn; it is much more amusing to run after butterflies or to climb trees."

"Poor little goose! Do you not know that you will grow up a perfect donkey and everyone will make fun of you?"

"Hold your tongue, you ugly creature!" shouted Pinocchio.

But the Cricket, who was patient and philosophical, instead of becoming angry at this impertinence, continued in the same tone. "If you do not wish to go to school, why not at least learn a trade – if only to enable you to earn honestly a piece of bread!"

"Do you want me to tell you?" replied Pinocchio, who was beginning to lose patience. "Amongst all the trades in the world there is only one that really takes my fancy."

"And that trade – what is it?"

"It is to eat, drink, sleep and amuse myself, and to wander about from morning to night."

"As a rule," said the Talking Cricket with the same composure, "all those who follow that trade end almost always either in a hospital or in prison."

"Take care! You'll be sorry if I get angry!"

"Poor Pinocchio! I really pity you!"

"Why do you pity me?"

"Because you are a puppet and, what is worse, because you have a wooden head."

At these last words Pinocchio jumped up in a rage and, snatching a wooden hammer from the bench, he threw it at the Talking Cricket.

Perhaps he never meant to hit him; but unfortunately it struck him exactly on the head. The poor Cricket had scarcely breath to cry, "Cri-cri-cri!" and there he was flattened against the wall.

Chapter 5

Pinocchio is hungry and searches for an egg to make himself an omelette;
but just at the most interesting moment, the omelette flies out of the window.

NIGHT was coming on and appetite began to gnaw in Pinocchio's stomach, reminding him that he had eaten nothing all day.

Poor Pinocchio ran quickly to the fireplace where a saucepan was boiling. He was going to take off the lid to see what was in it – but the saucepan was only painted on the wall! You can imagine how he felt! His nose, which was already long, became longer by at least three finger-lengths.

He then began to run about the room, searching in the drawers and in every imaginable place, in the hope of finding a bit of dry bread, a bone left by a dog, a little mouldy pudding of Indian corn, a fish bone, a cherry stone – anything that he could gnaw. But he could find nothing, nothing at all.

Meanwhile his hunger grew and grew… He began to cry desperately and he said: "The Talking Cricket was right. I did wrong to rebel against my papa and to run away from home… Oh, what a dreadful illness hunger is!"

Just then he thought he saw something in a heap of sweepings-up – something round and white that looked like a hen's egg. In a second he had sprung and seized hold of it. It was indeed an egg!

Pinocchio's joy cannot be described. Almost thinking he was dreaming, he kept turning the egg over in his hands, feeling it and kissing it. And as he kissed it he said: "Now, how shall I cook it? Shall I make an omelette? Or would it not be tastier fried in a frying-pan? Or shall I simply boil it? No, the quickest way of all is to scramble it in a saucepan: I am in such a hurry to eat it!"

Without losing a second, he placed an earthenware saucepan on a brazier full of red-hot embers. Into the saucepan instead of oil or butter he poured a little water; and when the water began to smoke – tac! – he broke the eggshell over it that the contents might drop in. But instead of the white and the yolk a little chicken popped out, very gay and polite! Making a beautiful curtsey it said to him: "A thousand thanks, Master Pinocchio, for saving me the trouble of breaking my shell. Adieu until we meet again!" Thus saying, it spread its wings, darted through the open window and flew away.

The poor puppet stood as if he had been bewitched, with his eyes fixed, his mouth open, and the eggshell in his hand. Coming to his senses, however, he began to cry and scream, and to stamp his feet on the floor in desperation. Amidst his sobs he said: "Ah! Indeed the Talking Cricket was right. If only I had not run away from home and my papa was here, I would not now be dying of hunger!"

And as his stomach cried out more than ever and he did not know how to quiet it, he thought he would leave the house and walk to the neighbours nearby in hopes of finding some charitable person who would give him a piece of bread.

Chapter 6

Pinocchio falls asleep with his feet on the brazier,
and wakes in the morning to find them burnt off.

I_T was a wild and stormy winter's night. The thunder was tremendous and the lightning so vivid that the sky seemed on fire. A bitter, blustery wind whistled angrily and, raising clouds of dust, swept over the country, causing the trees to creak and groan as it passed.

Pinocchio had a great fear of thunder, but his hunger was stronger than his fear. He made a rush for the village, which he reached in a hundred bounds, panting for breath.

He found it all dark and deserted. The shops were closed, the windows shut, and there was not so much as a dog in the street. It seemed the land of the dead.

Pinocchio, urged by desperation and hunger, laid hold of the bell of a house and began to ring it with all his might.

A little old man appeared at a window with a nightcap on his head, and called to him angrily: "What do you want at such an hour?"

"Would you be kind enough to give me a little bread?"

"Wait there, I will be back directly," said the little old man.

After half a minute the window was again opened and the little old man shouted: "Come underneath and hold out your cap."

Pinocchio pulled off his cap; but as he held it out, an enormous basin of water was poured down on him, watering him from head to foot as if he had been a pot of dried-up geraniums.

Chapter 6

He returned home like a wet chicken, quite exhausted with fatigue and hunger. No longer having the strength to stand, he sat down and rested his damp and muddy feet on a brazier full of burning embers to dry them. But then he fell asleep... and whilst he slept his feet, which were wooden, caught fire! Little by little they burnt away and became cinders. Pinocchio continued to sleep and to snore as if his feet belonged to someone else.

At last, about daybreak, he awoke because someone was knocking at the door.

"Who is there?" he asked, yawning and rubbing his eyes.

"It is I!" answered a voice.

The voice was Geppetto's.

Chapter 7

Geppetto returns home and gives Pinocchio the breakfast
that the poor man had brought for himself.

OOR Pinocchio, whose eyes were still half shut from sleep, had not as yet discovered that his feet were burnt off. The moment, therefore, that he heard his father's voice, he sprang off his stool to run and open the door – but after stumbling two or three times he fell headlong on the floor.

"Open the door!" shouted Geppetto from the street.

"Dear Papa, I cannot," answered the puppet, crying and rolling about on the ground. "My feet have been eaten!"

"Open the door, I tell you!" repeated Geppetto.

"I cannot stand up, believe me. Oh, poor me! I shall have to walk on my knees for the rest of my life!"

Geppetto, believing that all this wailing was only another of the puppet's tricks, thought how he could put a stop to it. He climbed up the wall and got in at the window.

He was very angry, but when he saw Pinocchio lying on the ground and really without feet, he was quite overcome. He took him in his arms and began to kiss him. Big tears ran down his cheeks as he said, sobbing: "My little Pinocchio! How did you manage to burn your feet?"

"I don't know, Papa, but believe me it has been an infernal night that I shall remember as long as I live. There was thunder and lightning, and I was very hungry, and I killed the Talking Cricket, but I

Chapter 7

didn't wish to kill him, and I put an earthenware saucepan on a brazier of burning embers, but a chicken flew out. And I got still more hungry, which is why that little old man opened his window and poured a basinful of water on my head. And I returned home and because I was still very hungry I put my feet on the brazier to dry them... And I am still hungry, but I have no longer any feet! Oh! Oh!..." And poor Pinocchio began to cry and to roar so loudly that he was heard five miles off.

Geppetto had from all this jumbled account understood only one thing: that the puppet was dying of hunger. He drew from his pocket three pears and gave them to Pinocchio, saying: "These three pears were intended for my breakfast, but I will give them to you gladly."

"If you wish me to eat them, be kind enough to peel them for me."

"Peel them?" said Geppetto, astonished. "I should never have thought, my boy, that you were so dainty and fussy. That is bad! In this world we should accustom ourselves from childhood to like and to eat everything, for there is no saying how we might end up. So much is down to chance!"

"I will never eat fruit that has not been peeled," interrupted Pinocchio. "I cannot bear peel."

Pinocchio

So good Geppetto fetched a knife and, arming himself with patience, peeled the three pears and put the pear skins on a corner of the table.

Having eaten the first pear in two mouthfuls, Pinocchio was about to throw away the core. But Geppetto caught hold of his arm and said to him: "Do not throw it away; in this world everything may be of use."

"I won't eat the core – I mean it!" shouted the puppet. And so Geppetto placed the three cores on the corner of the table together with the three pear skins.

Pinocchio yawned tremendously, and then said in a fretful tone: "I am as hungry as ever!"

"But, my boy, I have nothing more to give you!"

"Nothing? Really nothing?"

"Only the peelings and the cores of the three pears."

"Well, I suppose," said Pinocchio, "if there is nothing else, I will eat a pear skin."

And he began to chew it. At first he made a wry face; but then he quickly disposed of one peel after another, and after them even the cores, and when he had eaten up everything he clapped his hands on his sides in his satisfaction, and said joyfully: "Ah! Now I feel comfortable."

"You see now," observed Geppetto, "that I was right when I said to you that it did not do to accustom ourselves to be too particular or too dainty in our tastes. We can never know, my dear boy, what may happen to us. It is all down to chance!"

Chapter 8

*Geppetto makes Pinocchio new feet and sells his
own coat to buy him an ABC book.*

No sooner had the puppet appeased his hunger than he
began to cry and to grumble because he wanted a pair
of new feet. But Geppetto, to teach him a lesson after
being mischievous, allowed him to cry and despair for half the day.
He then said to him: "Why should I make you new feet? To enable
you, perhaps, to escape again from home?"

"I promise you," said the puppet, sobbing, "that I will go to school
and that I will study and earn a good character "

"All boys," replied Geppetto, "when they are bent upon obtaining
something, say the same thing."

"But I am not like other boys! I am better than all of them and I
always speak the truth. I promise you, Papa, that I will learn a trade,
and that I will be the comfort and support of your old age."

Although Geppetto put on a severe face, his eyes were full of tears
and his heart big with sorrow at seeing his poor Pinocchio in such a
pitiable state. He did not say another word but, taking his tools and
two small pieces of well-seasoned wood, he set to work with great
diligence. In less than an hour the feet were finished: two little feet
– swift, well-crafted and nimble.

Geppetto then, with a little glue which he had melted in an
eggshell, fastened his feet in place. It was so well done that not even a
trace could be seen of where they were joined.

Pinocchio

The puppet began to spring and caper about the room, as if he had gone mad with delight.

"To reward you for what you have done for me," said Pinocchio to his father, "I will go to school at once."

"Good boy."

"But to go to school, I shall need some clothes."

Geppetto, who was poor and who had not so much as a farthing in his pocket, then made him a little jacket of flowered paper, a pair of shoes from the bark of a tree, and a cap modelled from bread dough.

Pinocchio ran immediately to look at himself in a crock of water. He was so pleased with his appearance that he said, strutting about like a peacock: "I look quite like a gentleman!"

"Yes indeed," answered Geppetto, "but bear in mind that it is not fine clothes that make the gentleman, but rather clean clothes."

"By the bye," added the puppet, "in order to go to school I still need something else. I have no ABC book."

"You are right: but what shall we do to get one?"

"It is quite easy. We have only to go to the bookseller's and buy it."

"And the money?"

"I have not got any."

"Neither have I," added the good old man sadly.

And Pinocchio, although he was a very merry boy, became sad also; because poverty when it is real poverty is understood by everybody – even by boys.

Chapter 8

"Well, let's see!" exclaimed Geppetto, all at once rising to his feet. And, putting on his old workman's coat, all patched and darned, he ran out of the house.

He returned shortly, holding in his hand an ABC book for Pinocchio – but the old coat was gone. The poor man was in his shirt sleeves – and out-of-doors it was snowing.

"And the coat, Papa?"

"I have sold it."

"Why did you sell it?"

"Because I found it too hot."

Pinocchio understood this answer in an instant and, unable to restrain the impulse of his good heart he sprang up and, throwing his arms round Geppetto's neck, he began kissing him again and again.

Chapter 9

Pinocchio sells his ABC book, so he may
go and see a puppet show.

As soon as it had finished snowing, Pinocchio set out for school with his fine ABC book under his arm. Talking to himself, he said: "Today at school I will learn to read straight away; then tomorrow I will begin to write, and the day after tomorrow to do arithmetic. Then with my skills I will earn a great deal of money; and with the first money I have in my pocket I will immediately buy for my papa a beautiful new cloth coat. But what am I saying? Cloth, indeed! It shall be all made of gold and silver, and it shall have diamond buttons. That poor man really deserves it!"

Whilst he was saying this, he thought that he heard music in the distance that sounded like fifes and the beating of a big drum: fi-fi-fi, fi-fi-fi, zum, zum, zum, zum.

He stopped and listened. The sounds came from the end of a little street that led to a small village on the seashore.

"What can that music be? What a pity that I have to go to school, or else..."

And he stood, hesitating. Should he go to school? Or should he go after the fifes? He had to come to a decision.

"Today I will go and hear the fifes and tomorrow I will go to school," the young scamp finally decided, shrugging his shoulders.

The more he ran, the nearer came the sounds of the fifes and the beating of the big drum: fi-fi-fi, zum, zum, zum, zum.

Chapter 9

At last he found himself in the middle of a square quite full of people, who were all crowding round a building made of wood and canvas, and painted a thousand colours.

"What is that building?" asked Pinocchio, turning to a local little boy.

"Read the placard – it is all written – and then you will know."

"I would read it willingly, but it so happens that today I don't know how to read."

"Bravo, blockhead! Then I will read it to you. The writing on that placard in those letters red as fire is: 'GREAT PUPPET THEATRE'."

"Has the play already begun?"

"It is beginning now."

"How much does it cost to go in?"

"Twopence."

Pinocchio, who was in a fever of curiosity, lost all control of himself and, without any shame, he said to the little boy to whom he was talking: "Would you lend me twopence until tomorrow?"

"I would lend them to you willingly," said the other, making fun of him, "but it so happens that today I cannot give them to you."

"I will sell you my jacket for twopence," the puppet then said to him.

"What do you think that I could do with a jacket of flowered paper? If there was rain and it got wet, it would be impossible to get it off my back."

"Will you buy my shoes?"

"They would only be of use to light the fire."

"How much will you give me for my cap?"

"That would be a wonderful acquisition indeed! A cap of dough! There would be a risk of the mice coming to eat it whilst it was on my head."

Pinocchio felt agonised. He was on the point of making another offer, but he had not the courage. He hesitated, he wondered and he felt remorseful. At last he said: "Will you give me twopence for this new ABC book?"

"I am a boy and I don't buy from boys," replied Pinocchio's little acquaintance, who had much more sense than he had.

"I will buy the ABC book for twopence," called out a hawker of old clothes, who had been listening to the conversation.

And the book was sold there and then. And to think that poor Geppetto had remained at home trembling with cold in his shirt sleeves, that he might buy his son an ABC book!

Chapter 10

*The puppets recognise their brother Pinocchio and receive him
with delight; but at that moment their master, Fire-eater, makes his
appearance and Pinocchio is in danger of coming to a bad end.*

WHEN Pinocchio went into the little puppet theatre, the curtain was drawn up and the play had already begun. On the stage, Harlequin and Punchinello were, as usual, quarrelling with each other and threatening every moment to come to blows. The audience, all attention, laughed till their sides ached.

All at once Harlequin stopped short and, turning to the public, he pointed with his hand to someone far down in the pit, and exclaimed in a dramatic tone: "Gods of the firmament! Do I dream, or am I awake? But surely that is Pinocchio!"

"It is indeed Pinocchio!" cried Punchinello.

"It is indeed himself!" screamed Miss Rose, peeping from behind the scenes.

"It is Pinocchio! It is Pinocchio!" shouted all the puppets in chorus, leaping from all sides on to the stage. "It is Pinocchio! It is our brother Pinocchio! Long live Pinocchio!"

"Pinocchio, come up here to me," cried Harlequin, "and throw yourself into the arms of your wooden brothers!"

At this affectionate invitation, Pinocchio made a leap from the end of the pit into the reserved seats; another leap landed him on the head of the leader of the orchestra, and he then sprang upon the stage.

Chapter 10

It is impossible to describe the embraces, the hugs, the friendly pinches, and the demonstrations of warm brotherly affection that Pinocchio received from the excited crowd of actors and actresses of the puppet company.

The sight was doubtless a moving one, but the public in the pit, finding that the play was stopped, became impatient, and began to shout: "We will have the play – go on with the play!"

It was all wasted breath. The puppets, instead of continuing the recital, redoubled their noise and clamour and, putting Pinocchio on their shoulders, they carried him in triumph before the footlights.

At that moment, out came the showman. He was very big and so ugly that the sight of him was enough to frighten anyone. His beard was as black as ink and so long that it reached from his chin to the ground – he trod upon it when he walked! His mouth was as big as an oven and his eyes were like two lanterns of red glass with lights burning inside them. He carried a large whip made of snakes and foxes' tails twisted together, which he cracked constantly.

At his unexpected appearance there was a profound silence: no one dared to breathe. A fly might have been heard in the stillness. The poor puppets – both girls and boys – trembled like so many leaves.

"Why have you come to raise a disturbance in my theatre?" the showman asked Pinocchio, in the gruff voice of a hobgoblin suffering from a severe cold in the head.

"Believe me, honoured sir, that it was not my fault!"

"That is enough! Tonight we will settle our accounts."

As soon as the play was over, the showman went into the kitchen where a fine sheep was turning slowly on the spit in front of the fire, in preparation for his supper. As there was not enough wood to finish roasting and browning it, he called Harlequin and Punchinello, and said to them: "Bring that puppet here. It seems to me that he is made of very dry wood and I am sure that if he was thrown on the fire he would make a beautiful blaze for the roast."

At first Harlequin and Punchinello hesitated; but, frightened by a severe glance from their master, they obeyed. In a short time they returned to the kitchen carrying poor Pinocchio, who was wriggling like an eel taken out of water, and screaming desperately: "Papa! Papa! Save me! I don't want to die! I don't want to die!"

Chapter 11

The showman, Fire-eater, pardons Pinocchio and makes him a present of five gold pieces to take home to his father, Geppetto: but Pinocchio instead allows himself to be taken in by the Fox and the Cat, and goes with them.

THE showman, Fire-eater – for that was his name – looked, I must say, a terrible man, especially with his black beard that covered his chest and legs like an apron. On the whole, however, he had not a bad heart. In proof of this, when he saw poor Pinocchio brought before him, struggling and screaming "I don't want to die! I don't want to die!" he was quite moved and felt very sorry for him. He tried to hold out, but after a little he could stand it no longer and he sneezed violently.

When he heard the sneeze, Harlequin, who up to that moment had been as sorrowful and drooping as a weeping willow, became quite cheerful. Leaning towards Pinocchio, he whispered to him softly: "Good news, brother. The showman has sneezed – that is a sign that he pities you and, consequently, you are saved."

For you must know that Fire-eater, whenever he was really overcome, had the habit of sneezing.

After he had sneezed, the showman, still acting the ruffian, shouted to Pinocchio: "Have done crying! Your wailing has given me a pain in my stomach... Atchoo! Atchoo!" and he sneezed again twice.

"Bless you!" said Pinocchio.

"Thank you! And your papa and your mamma, are they still alive?" asked Fire-eater.

Pinocchio

"Papa, yes: my mamma I have never known."

"Who can say what a sorrow it would be for your poor old father if I was to have you thrown amongst those burning coals! Atchoo! Atchoo! Atchoo!" and he sneezed again three times.

"Bless you!" said Pinocchio.

"Thank you! What is your father's name?"

"Geppetto."

"And what trade does he follow?"

"He is a wood carver."

"Does he earn much?"

"Earn much? Why, he has never a penny in his pocket. Only think, to buy an ABC book for me to go to school, he was obliged to sell the only coat he had to wear – a coat that between patches and darns was not fit to be seen."

"Poor devil! I feel sorry for him! Here are five gold pieces. Go at once and take them to him with my compliments."

Pinocchio thanked the showman a thousand times. He embraced all the puppets of the company one by one and set out to return home, beside himself with delight.

He had not gone far when he met on the road a Fox, who was lame in one foot, and a Cat, who was blind in both eyes, who were helping each other along like good companions in misfortune.

"Good day, Pinocchio," said the Fox, greeting him politely.

"How do you come to know my name?" asked the puppet.

"I know your father well. I saw him yesterday at the door of his house, in his shirt sleeves and shivering with cold."

"Poor Papa! But that is over; for the future he shall shiver no more!"

"Why?"

"Because I have become a gentleman."

"A gentleman – you?" said the Fox, and he began to laugh rudely and scornfully. The Cat also began to laugh, but to conceal it she

combed her whiskers with her forepaws.

"There is little to laugh at," cried Pinocchio angrily. "You can see that these here are five gold pieces." And he pulled out the money of which Fire-eater had made him a present.

At the merry chink of the money, the Fox, without thinking, stretched out the paw that had seemed crippled, and the Cat opened wide two eyes that looked like two green lanterns. However, she shut them again so quickly that Pinocchio observed nothing.

"I intend to buy a new coat for my papa, made of gold and silver, and with diamond buttons," said the puppet, "and then I will buy an ABC book for myself, for I wish to go to school to study in earnest."

"Look at me!" said the Fox. "Through my foolish passion for study I have lost a leg."

"Look at me!" said the Cat. "Through my foolish passion for study I have lost the sight of both my eyes."

At that moment a white Blackbird, that was perched on the hedge by the road, began his usual song, and said: "Pinocchio, don't listen to the advice of bad companions: if you do, you will repent it!"

Poor Blackbird – if only he had not spoken! The Cat, with a great leap, sprang upon him and, without even giving him time to say 'Oh!' ate him in a mouthful, feathers and all.

Having eaten him and cleaned her mouth, she shut her eyes again and feigned blindness as before.

"Poor Blackbird!" said Pinocchio to the Cat. "Why did you treat him so badly?"

"I did it to teach him a lesson. He will learn another time not to meddle in other people's conversation."

They had gone almost halfway when the Fox, halting suddenly, said to the puppet: "Would you like to double your money? Would you like to make out of your five sovereigns, a hundred, a thousand, two thousand?"

Chapter 11

"I should think so! But in what way?"

"The way is easy enough. Instead of returning home, you must go with us."

"And where do you wish to take me?"

"To the City of Fools."

Pinocchio reflected a moment, and then he said resolutely: "No, I will not go. I am already close to the house, and I will return home to my papa who is waiting for me. I have indeed been a bad son."

"Well, then," said the Fox, "go then, but you'll be sorry."

"You'll be sorry," repeated the Cat.

"Think well of it, Pinocchio, for you are turning your back on fortune."

"On fortune!" repeated the Cat.

"Between today and tomorrow your five sovereigns would have become two thousand."

"Two thousand!" repeated the Cat.

"But how is it possible that they could have become so many?" asked Pinocchio, remaining with his mouth open from astonishment.

"I will explain it to you at once," said the Fox. "You must know that in the City of Fools there is a sacred field called by everybody the Field of Miracles. In this field you must dig a little hole and you put into it, we will say, one gold sovereign. You then cover up the hole with a little earth. You must water it with two pails of water from the fountain. Then sprinkle it with two pinches of salt, and when night comes you can go quietly to bed. In the meanwhile, during the night, the gold piece will grow and flower, and in the morning when you get up and return to the field, what do you find? You find a beautiful tree laden with two thousand five hundred shining gold sovereigns."

"Oh! How delightful!" cried Pinocchio, dancing for joy. "As soon as ever I have obtained those sovereigns, I will keep two thousand for myself, and the other five hundred I will make a present of to you two."

"A present to us?" cried the Fox with indignation, and appearing much offended. "Don't even consider it!"

"Don't even consider it!" repeated the Cat.

"We do not work," said the Fox, "to make money ourselves: we work solely to enrich others."

"Others!" repeated the Cat.

'What good people!' thought Pinocchio to himself. Forgetting there and then his papa, the new coat, the ABC book, and all his good resolutions, he said to the Fox and the Cat: "Let us be off at once. I will go with you."

Chapter 12

The inn of the Red Lobster.

THEY walked, and walked, and walked, until at last, towards evening, they arrived dead tired at the inn of the Red Lobster.

"Let us stop here a little," said the Fox, "so that we may have something to eat and rest ourselves for an hour or two. We will start again at midnight, so as to arrive at the Field of Miracles by dawn tomorrow morning."

Having gone into the inn, they all three sat down at a table: but none of them had any appetite.

The Cat, who was suffering from indigestion and feeling seriously unwell, could only eat thirty-five mullet with tomato sauce and four portions of tripe with Parmesan cheese; and because she thought the tripe was not seasoned enough, she asked three times for the butter and grated cheese!

The Fox would also willingly have picked a little, but as his doctor had ordered him a strict diet, he was forced to content himself simply with a hare dressed with a sweet-and-sour sauce, and garnished lightly with fat chickens and early pullets. After the hare he sent for a dish of partridges, rabbits, frogs, lizards, and other delicacies; he could not touch anything else. He had such a disgust to food, he said, that he could put nothing to his lips.

The one who ate the least was Pinocchio. He asked for some walnuts and a hunk of bread, and left everything on his plate. The poor boy, whose thoughts were continually fixed on the Field of

Pinocchio

Miracles, had got an indigestion of gold pieces.

When they had had supper, the Fox said to the host: "Give us two good rooms, one for Mr Pinocchio, and the other for me and my companion. We will snatch a little sleep before we leave. Remember, however, that at midnight we wish to be called to continue our journey."

"Yes, gentlemen," answered the host, and he winked at the Fox and the Cat as much as to say:

'I know what you are up to. We understand one another!'

No sooner had Pinocchio got into bed than he fell asleep at once and began to dream. And he dreamt that he was in the middle of a field full of shrubs covered with clusters of gold sovereigns. But just as Pinocchio was stretching out his hand to pick handfuls of those beautiful gold pieces and to put them in his pocket, he was suddenly wakened by three violent blows on the door of his room. It was the host who had come to tell him that midnight had struck.

"Are my companions ready?" asked the puppet.

"Ready! Why, they left two hours ago."

"Why were they in such a hurry?"

"Because the Cat had received a message to say that her eldest kitten was ill with chilblains on his feet and was in danger of death."

"Did they pay for the supper?"

"What are you thinking of? They are much too well educated to dream of offering such an insult to a gentleman like you."

"What a pity! It is an insult that would have given me so much pleasure!" said Pinocchio, scratching his head. He then asked: "And where did my good friends say they would wait for me?"

"At the Field of Miracles, tomorrow morning at daybreak."

Pinocchio paid a sovereign for his supper and that of his companions, and then left.

Outside the inn it was so pitch dark that he had almost to grope his way, for it was impossible to see a hand's breadth in front of him. As he was walking along he saw a little insect shining dimly on the trunk of a tree, like a night light in a lamp of transparent china.

"Who are you?" asked Pinocchio.

"I am the ghost of the Talking Cricket," answered the insect in a low voice, so weak and faint that it seemed to come from the other world. "I want to give you some advice. Go back, and take the four sovereigns that you have left to your poor father, who is weeping and in despair because you have never returned to him."

"By tomorrow my papa will be a gentleman, for these four sovereigns will have become two thousand."

"Don't trust, my boy, to those who promise to make you rich in a day. Usually they are either mad or rogues! Listen to me and go back."

"On the contrary, I am determined to go on."

"The hour is late!"

"I am determined to go on."

"The night is dark!"

"I am determined to go on."

"The road is dangerous!"

"I am determined to go on."

"Remember that boys who are determined to have their own way sooner or later repent it."

"Always the same stories. Goodnight, Cricket."

"Goodnight, Pinocchio, and may Heaven preserve you."

No sooner had he said these words than the Talking Cricket vanished suddenly like a light that has been blown out, and the road became darker than ever.

Chapter 13

*Pinocchio, because he would not heed the good advice
of the Talking Cricket, falls amongst outlaws.*

As Pinocchio resumed his journey, he thought that he heard a slight rustle of leaves behind him. He turned to look, and saw in the gloom two evil-looking black figures, completely enveloped in coal sacks. They were running after him on tiptoe and making great leaps like two phantoms.

"Here they are in real life!" he said to himself and, not knowing where to hide his gold pieces, he put them in his mouth, tucked under his tongue. Then he tried to escape. But he had not gone a step when he felt himself seized by the arm and heard two horrid ghoulish voices saying to him: "Your money or your life!"

Pinocchio, not being able to answer in words, owing to the money that was in his mouth, made a thousand low bows and a thousand silent gestures. He tried thus to make the two muffled figures, whose eyes were only visible through the holes in their sacks, understand that he was a poor puppet, and that he had not as much as a false farthing in his pocket.

"Come now! Less nonsense and out with the money!" cried the two outlaws threateningly.

And the puppet made a gesture with his hands to signify: 'I have got none.'

"Deliver up your money or you are dead," said the tallest of the outlaws.

"Dead!" repeated the other. "And after we have killed you, we will also kill your father."

"Also your father!"

"No, no, no, not my poor papa!" cried Pinocchio in a despairing tone, and as he said it, the sovereigns clinked in his mouth.

"Ah! You rascal! Then you have hidden your money under your tongue!"

One of them seized the puppet by the end of his nose, and the other took him by the chin, and they began to pull them brutally, the one up and the other down, to force him to open his mouth. But Pinocchio, as quick as lightning, caught one outlaw's hand with his teeth, and with one bite ripped it clean off and spat it out. Imagine his astonishment when, instead of a hand, he perceived that he had spat a cat's paw on to the ground.

Encouraged by this first victory, Pinocchio used his nails to such purpose that he succeeded in freeing himself from his attackers and, jumping the hedge by the roadside, he began to fly across country. The outlaws ran after him like two dogs chasing a hare: and the one who had lost a paw ran on one leg, and no one ever knew how he managed it.

Pinocchio raced across fields and vineyards. The outlaws followed him and kept behind him without once giving in.

The day began to break and still they pursued him. Suddenly Pinocchio found his way barred by a wide, deep ditch full of dirty water the colour of coffee. What was he to do? "One! Two! Three!" cried the puppet and, making a rush, he sprang to the other side. The outlaws also jumped but, not having measured the distance properly – Splash! – they fell into the very middle of the ditch. Pinocchio, who heard the plunge and the splashing of the water, shouted out, laughing, and without stopping: "Enjoy your bath, gentleman outlaws."

And he felt convinced that they were drowned when, turning to

look, he perceived that on the contrary they were both running after
him, still enveloped in their sacks, with the water dripping from them
as if they had been two hollow baskets.

Chapter 14

The outlaws pursue Pinocchio and, having overtaken him, hang him to a branch of the Big Oak.

A T this sight the puppet's courage failed him; he was on the point of throwing himself on the ground and giving himself up for lost once again. However, turning his eyes in every direction, he saw at some distance, standing out amidst the dark green of the trees, a small house as white as snow. And without delaying an instant, he began again running for his life through the wood, with the outlaws after him.

At last, after a desperate race of nearly two hours, he arrived quite breathless at the door of the house and knocked very hard, for he heard the sound of steps approaching him and the heavy panting of his persecutors.

There was no answer.

He began in desperation to kick and pummel the door with all his might.

The window then opened and a beautiful child appeared at it. She had blue hair and a face as white as a waxwork; and her hands were crossed on her breast. Without moving her lips in the least, she said in a voice that seemed to come from the other world: "In this house there is no one. They are all dead."

Chapter 14

"Then at least open the door for me yourself," shouted Pinocchio, crying and imploring.

"I am dead also."

"Dead? Then what are you doing there at the window?"

"I am waiting for the bier to come to carry me away."

Having said this she immediately disappeared, and the window was closed again without the slightest noise.

"Oh! Beautiful child with blue hair," cried Pinocchio, "open the door! Have compassion on a poor boy pursued by outla—"

But he could not finish the word, for he felt himself seized by the collar and the same two horrible voices said to him threateningly: "You shall not escape from us again!"

The puppet, seeing death staring him in the face, was taken with such a violent fit of trembling that the joints of his wooden legs began to creak and the sovereigns hidden under his tongue to clink.

"Now then," demanded the outlaws, "this time we will force you to open your mouth!"

"I see what we must do," said one of them. "He must be hanged! Let us hang him!"

"Let us hang him!" repeated the other.

Without losing any time they tied Pinocchio's arms behind him, passed a running noose round his throat and hung him to the branch of a tree called the Big Oak.

They then sat down on the grass and waited for his last struggle. But the puppet kept his eyes open, his mouth closed, and kicked more than ever.

Losing patience, they turned to Pinocchio and said in a bantering tone: "Goodbye till tomorrow. Let us hope that when we return you will be polite enough to allow yourself to be found quite dead and with your mouth wide open."

And they walked off.

Chapter 15

The beautiful child with blue hair has the
puppet taken down and put to bed.

WHILST poor Pinocchio swung from a branch of the
Big Oak, the beautiful child with blue hair came again
to the window. When she saw the unhappy puppet
hanging by his throat, and dancing up and down in the gusts of the
north wind, she was moved with compassion. Striking her hands
together, she gave three little claps.

At this signal there came a sound of the sweep of wings flying
rapidly, and a large Falcon flew on to the windowsill.

"What are your orders, gracious Fairy?" he asked, inclining his beak
in sign of reverence – for I must tell you that the child with blue hair
was no more and no less than a beautiful Fairy, who for more than a
thousand years had lived in the wood.

"Do you see that puppet dangling from a branch of the Big Oak?"

"I see him."

"Very well. Fly there at once. With your strong beak, break the knot
that keeps him suspended in the air and lay him gently on the grass at
the foot of the tree."

The Falcon flew away and after two minutes he returned, saying: "I
have done as you commanded."

The Fairy then, striking her hands together, made two little claps –
and a magnificent Poodle appeared, walking upright on his hind legs
exactly as if he had been a man.

Chapter 15

He was in the full-dress livery of a coachman. On his head he had a three-cornered cap braided with gold, his curly white wig came down on to his shoulders, he had a chocolate-coloured waistcoat with diamond buttons, and two large pockets to contain the bones that his mistress gave him at dinner. He had as well a pair of short crimson velvet breeches, silk stockings, low-styled shoes and, hanging behind him, a type of umbrella-case made of blue satin, to put his tail into when the weather was rainy.

"Be quick, Medoro, like a good dog!" said the Fairy to the Poodle. "Have the most beautiful carriage in my coach-house prepared and take the road to the wood. When you come to the Big Oak you will find a poor puppet stretched on the grass, half dead. Pick him up gently and lay him flat on the cushions of the carriage and bring him here to me. Have you understood?"

The Poodle, to show that he had understood, shook the case of blue satin that he had on three or four times, and ran off like a racehorse.

Shortly afterwards, a beautiful little carriage came out of the coach-house. The cushions were stuffed with canary feathers and the carriage was lined in the inside with whipped cream, custard and Savoy biscuits. The little carriage was drawn by a hundred pairs of white mice and the Poodle, seated on the coach-box, cracked his whip from side to side like a driver when he is afraid that he is behind time.

A quarter of an hour had not even passed when the carriage returned. The Fairy, who was waiting at the door of the house, took the poor puppet in her arms and carried him into a little room with mother-of-pearl walls and laid him in bed.

Chapter 16

Pinocchio will not take his medicine: when, however, he sees the grave-diggers who have arrived to carry him away, he takes it. He then tells a lie and, as a punishment, his nose grows longer.

THE Fairy approached Pinocchio and, having touched his forehead, she perceived that he was burning with a high fever. She therefore dissolved a certain white powder in half a tumbler of water and, offering it to the puppet, she said to him lovingly: "Drink it, and in a few days you will be cured."

Pinocchio looked at the tumbler, made a wry face, and then asked in a plaintive voice: "Is it sweet or bitter?"

"It is bitter, but it will do you good."

"If it is bitter, I will not take it. I don't like anything bitter."

"Drink it, and when you have drunk it I will give you a lump of sugar to take away the taste."

"Where is the lump of sugar?"

"Here it is," said the Fairy, taking a piece from a gold sugar-basin.

"Give me first the lump of sugar and then I will drink that bad bitter water..."

"Do you promise?"

"Yes..."

The Fairy gave him the sugar and Pinocchio, having crunched it up and swallowed it in a second, said, licking his lips: "It would be a fine thing if sugar was medicine! I would take it every day."

"Now keep your promise and drink these few drops of water,

which will restore you to health."

Pinocchio took the tumbler unwillingly in his hand and put the point of his nose to it. He then raised it to his lips. He then again put his nose to it, and at last said: "It is too bitter! Too bitter! I cannot drink it. I know it from the smell. I want first another lump of sugar – and then I will drink it!"

The Fairy then, with all the patience of a good mother, put another lump of sugar in his mouth, and then again presented the tumbler to him.

"I cannot drink it so!" said the puppet, making a thousand grimaces.

"Why?"

"Because that pillow that is down there on my feet bothers me."

The Fairy removed the pillow.

"It is useless. Even so I cannot drink it..."

"What is the matter now?"

"The door of the room, which is half open, bothers me."

The Fairy went and closed the door.

"In short," cried Pinocchio, bursting into tears, "I will not drink that bitter water – no, no, no!"

"My boy, you will be sorry..."

"I don't care..."

"Your illness is serious..."

"I don't care..."

"In a few hours, the fever will carry you into the other world..."

At that moment, the door of the room flew open and four rabbits as black as ink entered, carrying on their shoulders a little bier.

"What do you want with me?" cried Pinocchio, sitting up in bed in a great fright.

"We have come to take you," said the biggest rabbit.

"To take me? But I am not yet dead!"

Chapter 16

"No, not yet: but you have only a few minutes to live, as you have refused the medicine that would have cured you of the fever."

"Oh, Fairy, Fairy!" the puppet then began to scream. "Give me the tumbler at once. Be quick, for pity's sake, for I don't want to die – no, I don't want to die…" And taking the tumbler in both hands, he emptied it at a draught.

"Never mind!" said the rabbits. "This time we have made our journey in vain." And, taking the little bier again on their shoulders they left the room, grumbling and murmuring between their teeth.

In fact, a few minutes afterwards, Pinocchio jumped down from the bed quite well: because you must know that wooden puppets have the advantage of being seldom ill and of being cured very quickly.

"Oh! But another time I shall not require so much persuasion to take my medicine," cried Pinocchio. "I shall remember those black rabbits with the bier on their shoulders and then I shall immediately take the tumbler in my hand, and down it will go!"

"Now come here to me," urged the Fairy, "and tell me how it came about that you fell into the hands of those outlaws."

So Pinocchio told his story and, when he had finished, the Fairy asked: "The four pieces – where have you put them?"

"I have lost them!" said Pinocchio; but he was telling a lie, for he had them in his pocket.

He had scarcely told the lie when his nose, which was already long, grew at once two fingers longer.

"And where did you lose them?

"In the wood near here."

At this second lie his nose went on growing.

"If you have lost them in the wood near here," said the Fairy, "we will look for them, and we shall find them."

"Ah! Now I remember all about it," replied the puppet, getting quite confused; "I didn't lose the four gold pieces, I swallowed them inadvertently whilst I was drinking your medicine."

At this third lie his nose grew to such an extraordinary length that poor Pinocchio could not move in any direction. If he turned to one side he struck his nose against the bed or the windowpanes; if he turned to the other he struck it against the walls or the door; if he raised his head a little he ran the risk of sticking it into one of the Fairy's eyes.

And the Fairy looked at him and laughed.

"What are you laughing at?" asked the puppet, very confused and anxious at finding his nose so wondrously growing.

"I am laughing at the lie you have told."

Pinocchio, not knowing where to hide himself for shame, tried to run out of the room; but he did not succeed, for his nose had increased so much that it could no longer pass through the door.

Chapter 17

Pinocchio meets again the Fox and the Cat, and goes with them to bury his money in the Field of Miracles.

To teach Pinocchio a lesson, the Fairy allowed the puppet to cry and to wail for a good half-hour over his nose, which could no longer pass through the door of the room. Then she beat her hands together and at that signal a thousand large birds called woodpeckers flew in at the window. They immediately perched on Pinocchio's nose, and began to peck at it with such zeal that in a few minutes his enormous and ridiculous nose was reduced to its usual dimensions.

"What a good Fairy you are," said the puppet, drying his eyes, "and how much I love you!"

"I love you also," answered the Fairy. "If you will stay with me, you shall be my little brother and I will be your good little sister."

"I would stay willingly – but what about my poor papa?"

"I have thought of everything. I have already let your father know and he will be here tonight."

"Really?" shouted Pinocchio, jumping for joy. "Then, little Fairy, if you consent, I should like to go and meet him. I am so anxious to give a kiss to that poor old man who has suffered so much on my account, that I am counting the minutes."

"Go, then, but be careful not to get lost. Take the road through the wood and I am sure that you will meet him."

Pinocchio set out and as soon as he was in the wood he began to

Chapter 17

run like a kid. But when he had reached a certain spot, almost in front of the Big Oak, he stopped, because he thought that he heard people amongst the bushes. In fact, two persons came out on to the road. Can you guess who they were? His two travelling companions, the Fox and the Cat, with whom he had had supper at the inn of the Red Lobster.

"Why, here is our dear Pinocchio!" cried the Fox, kissing and embracing him. "How do you come to be here?"

"How do you come to be here?" repeated the Cat.

"It is a long story," answered the puppet, "which I will tell you when I have time."

Whilst they were thus talking, Pinocchio observed that the Cat had a lame front right leg, for in fact she had lost her paw with all its claws. He therefore asked her: "What have you done with your paw?"

The Cat tried to answer but became confused. Therefore the Fox said immediately: "My friend is too modest, which is why she does not speak. I will answer for her. I must tell you that an hour ago we met an old wolf on the road, almost fainting from want of food, who came begging from us. Not having so much as a fish bone to give him, what did my big-hearted friend do? She bit off one of her forepaws and threw it to that poor beast, so that he might ease his hunger." And the Fox, in relating this, dried a tear.

Pinocchio was also touched and, approaching the Cat, he whispered into her ear: "If all cats resembled you, how fortunate the mice would be!"

"And now, what are you doing here?" asked the Fox of the puppet.

"I am waiting for my papa, whom I expect to arrive every moment."

"And your gold pieces?"

"I have got them in my pocket – all but one that I spent at the inn of the Red Lobster."

"And to think that, instead of four pieces, by tomorrow they might become thousands! Why do you not listen to my advice? Why will you not go and bury them in the Field of Miracles?"

"Today it is impossible: I will go another day."

"Another day it will be too late!" said the Fox.

"Why?"

"Because the field has been bought by a gentleman and after tomorrow no one will be allowed to bury money there."

"How far off is the Field of Miracles?"

"Not two miles. Will you come with us? In half an hour you will be there. You can bury your money at once and in a few minutes you will collect two thousand, and this evening you will return with your pockets full. Will you come with us?"

Pinocchio thought of the good Fairy, old Geppetto, and the warnings of the Talking Cricket, and he hesitated a little before answering. He ended, however, by doing as all boys do who have not a grain of sense and who have no heart – he ended by giving his head a little shake, and saying to the Fox and the Cat: "Let's go: I will come with you."

And they went.

They walked for half the day and finally reached the town that was called the City of Fools. As soon as Pinocchio entered this town, he saw that the streets were crowded with dogs who had lost their coats and who were yawning from hunger, shorn sheep trembling with cold, cocks without combs or crests who were begging for a grain of Indian corn, large butterflies who could no longer fly because they had sold their beautiful coloured wings, peacocks who had no tails and were ashamed to be seen, and pheasants who went scratching about in a subdued fashion, mourning for their brilliant gold and silver feathers gone for ever.

In the midst of this crowd of beggars and shame-faced creatures, lordly carriages passed from time to time, each containing a Fox, or a thieving Magpie, or some other ravenous bird of prey.

"And where is the Field of Miracles?" asked Pinocchio.

"It is here, not two steps from us."

They crossed the town and, having gone beyond the walls, they came to a solitary field which to look at resembled all other fields.

"We are here," said the Fox to the puppet. "Now stoop down and dig with your hands a little hole in the ground and put your gold pieces into it."

Pinocchio obeyed. He dug a hole, put into it the four gold pieces that he had left, and then filled up the hole with a little earth.

"Now, then," said the Fox, "go to that nearby canal, fetch a can of water, and water the ground where you have sowed them."

Pinocchio went to the canal and, as he had no can, he took off one of his old shoes and filled it with water, then watered the ground over the hole.

He then asked: "Is there anything else to be done?"

"Nothing else," answered the Fox. "We can now go away. You can return in about twenty minutes and you will find a shrub already pushing through the ground, with its branches quite loaded with money."

The poor puppet, beside himself with joy, thanked the Fox and the Cat a thousand times, and promised them a beautiful present.

"We wish for no presents," answered the two rascals. "It is enough for us to have taught you the way to increase your wealth yourself without hard work. We are as happy as folk out for a holiday."

Thus saying, they took leave of Pinocchio and, wishing him a good harvest, went about their business.

Chapter 18

Pinocchio is robbed of his money and, as a punishment for the disobedience that led to this situation, he is sent to prison for four months.

THE puppet returned to the town and began to count the minutes, one by one. When he thought that it must be time, he took the road leading to the Field of Miracles. And as he walked along with hurried steps his heart beat fast – tic, tac, tic, tac – like a drawing-room clock when it is really going well. Meanwhile he was thinking to himself: 'And if instead of a thousand gold pieces, I was to find on the branches of the tree two thousand? And instead of two thousand, supposing I found five thousand? And instead of five thousand that I found a hundred thousand? Oh, what a fine gentleman I should then become! I would have a beautiful palace, a thousand little wooden horses and a thousand stables to amuse myself with, a cellar full of currant-wine and sweet syrups, and a library quite full of candies, tarts, plum-cakes, macaroons, and biscuits with cream.'

Whilst he was building these castles in the air he had arrived in the neighbourhood of the field, and he stopped to look if by chance he could perceive a tree with its branches laden with money – but he saw nothing. He advanced another hundred steps – nothing. He entered the field... He went right up to the little hole where he had buried his sovereigns – and nothing. He then became very thoughtful and, forgetting the rules of society and good manners, he took his hands out of his pockets and gave his head a long scratch.

Chapter 18

At that moment he heard an explosion of laughter close to him and, looking up, he saw a large Parrot perched on a tree, who was preening the few feathers he had left.

"Why are you laughing?" asked Pinocchio in an angry voice.

"I am laughing because in preening my feathers I tickled myself under my wings."

The puppet did not answer, but went to the canal and, filling the same old shoe full of water, he proceeded again to water the earth that covered his gold pieces.

Whilst he was thus occupied another laugh, still more impertinent than the first, rang out in the silence of that solitary place.

"Once and for all," shouted Pinocchio in a rage, "may I know, you ignorant Parrot, what you are laughing at?"

"I am laughing at those simpletons who believe in all the foolish things they are told, and who allow themselves to be trapped by those who are more cunning than they are."

"Are you perhaps speaking of me?"

"Yes, I am speaking of you, poor Pinocchio - of you who are simple enough to believe that money can be sown and gathered in fields in the same way as beans and squashes. I also believed it once and how I am suffering for it. Today - although it is too late - I have at last learnt that to put a few pennies honestly together it is necessary to earn them, either by the work of our own hands or by the cleverness of our own brains."

"I don't understand you," said the puppet, who was already trembling with fear.

"Have patience! I will explain myself better," insisted the Parrot. "You must know, then, that whilst you were in the town the Fox and the Cat returned to the field: they took the buried money and then fled like the wind. It will take a clever man to catch them!"

Pinocchio stood with his mouth open and, not choosing to believe the Parrot's words, he began with his hands and nails to dig up the earth that he had watered. And he dug, and dug, and dug, and made such a deep hole that a haystack might have stood upright in it: but the money was no longer there.

He rushed back to the town in a state of desperation and went at once to the Courts of Justice to report the two rogues who had robbed him to the judge.

The judge was a big ape of the gorilla tribe – an old ape respectable for his age, his white beard, and especially for his gold spectacles from which the glass had dropped out. He was always obliged to wear them on account of an inflammation of the eyes that had tormented him for many years.

Pinocchio related in the presence of the judge all the particulars of the infamous fraud of which he had been the victim. He gave the names, the surnames, and other details of the two rascals, and ended by demanding justice.

The judge listened with great kindness. He took a lively interest in the story and was much touched and moved. And when the puppet had nothing further to say, he stretched out his hand and rang a bell.

At this summons, two mastiffs immediately appeared dressed as officers. The judge then, pointing to Pinocchio, said to them: "That poor devil has been robbed of four gold pieces; take him and put him immediately into prison."

The puppet was petrified on hearing this unexpected sentence and tried to protest; but the officers, to avoid losing time, gagged him and carried him off to the lock-up. And there Pinocchio remained for four months – four long months.

Chapter 19

Liberated from prison, Pinocchio starts to return to the
Fairy's house; but on the road he meets with a horrible Serpent
and afterwards he is caught in a trap.

You can imagine Pinocchio's joy when he was finally freed. Without stopping to take breath, he immediately left the town and took the road that led to the Fairy's house.

On account of the rainy weather, the road had become a marsh into which he sank knee-deep. But the puppet would not give in. Tormented by the desire of seeing his father and his little sister with blue hair again he ran and leapt like a greyhound, and as he ran he was splashed with mud from head to foot. And he said to himself as he went along: "How many misfortunes have happened to me – and I deserved them! For I am an obstinate, stupid puppet. I am always bent upon having my own way, without listening to those who wish me well, and who have a thousand times more sense than I have! But from this time forth, I am determined to change and to become orderly and obedient."

Whilst he was saying this he stopped suddenly, frightened to death, and took four steps backwards.

What had he seen?

He had seen an immense Serpent stretched across the road! Its skin was green; it had red eyes and a pointed tail that was smoking like a chimney.

It's impossible to imagine the puppet's terror. He walked away to a

safe distance and, sitting down on a heap of stones, set about waiting until the Serpent went about its business and left the road clear.

He waited an hour; two hours; three hours; but the Serpent was always there. And even from a distance Pinocchio could see the red light of his fiery eyes and the column of smoke that ascended from the end of his tail.

At last Pinocchio, trying to feel courageous, approached to within a few steps and said to the Serpent in a little, soft, soothing voice: "Excuse me, Sir Serpent, but would you be so good as to move a little to one side, just enough to allow me to pass?"

He might as well have spoken to the wall. The Serpent did not move.

He began again in the same soft voice: "You must know, Sir Serpent, that I am on my way home, where my father is waiting for me, and it is such a long time since I saw him last! Will you therefore allow me to continue my journey?"

He waited for a sign in answer to this request, but there was none. In fact the Serpent, who up to that moment had been sprightly and full of life, became motionless and almost rigid. He shut his eyes and his tail ceased smoking.

"Can he really be dead?" said Pinocchio, rubbing his hands with delight; and he determined to jump over him and reach the other side of the road. But just as he was going to leap, the Serpent raised himself suddenly on end, like a spring set in motion. The puppet, drawing back in his terror, caught his feet and fell to the ground. He fell so awkwardly, his head stuck in the mud and his legs went into the air.

At the sight of the puppet kicking violently with his head in the mud, the Serpent went into convulsions of laughter, and he laughed, and laughed, until from the violence of his laughter he burst a blood-vessel in his chest and died. And that time he was really dead.

Pinocchio then set off running, in the hope that he should reach the Fairy's house before dark. But before long he began to suffer so dreadfully from hunger that he could not bear it. He jumped into a field by the wayside, intending to pick some bunches of muscatel grapes. Oh, that he had never done it! He had scarcely reached the vines when – Crack! His legs were caught between two cutting iron bars, and he became so giddy with pain that stars of every colour danced before his eyes.

The poor puppet had been snared in a trap put there to capture some big polecats who were the scourge of the poultry-yards in the neighbourhood.

Chapter 20

*Pinocchio is taken by a farmer, who forces him to fill
the place of his watchdog in the poultry-yard.*

PINOCCHIO, as you can imagine, began to cry and scream: but
his tears and groans were useless, for there was not a house to
be seen, and not a living soul passed down the road.

At last night came on.

Partly from the pain of the trap that cut his legs, and a little from
fear at finding himself alone in the dark in the midst of the fields, the
puppet was on the point of fainting.

Just at that moment he saw a Firefly flitting over his head. He
called to it and said: "Oh, little Firefly, will you have pity on me and
set me free from this torture?"

"Poor boy!" said the Firefly, stopping and looking at him with
compassion. "But how could your legs have been caught by those
sharp irons?"

"I came into the field to pick two bunches of these muscatel
grapes, and–"

"But were the grapes yours?"

"No..."

"Then who taught you to carry off other people's property?"

"I was so hungry..."

"Hunger, my boy, is not a good reason for taking what does not
belong to us..."

"That is true!" said Pinocchio, crying. "I will never do it again."

Chapter 20

At this moment their conversation was interrupted by the light sound of approaching footsteps. It was the owner of the field coming on tiptoe to see if one of the polecats that ate his chickens during the night had been caught in his trap.

When, having brought out his lantern from under his coat, he perceived that instead of a polecat a boy had been taken, he was greatly astonished.

"Ah, little thief!" said the angry farmer. "Then it is you who is carrying off my chickens?"

"No, it is not I; indeed it is not!" cried Pinocchio, sobbing. "I only came into the field to take two bunches of grapes!"

"He who steals grapes is quite capable of stealing chickens. Leave it to me, I will give you a lesson that you will not forget in a hurry."

Opening the trap, he seized the puppet by the collar and carried him to his house as if he had been a young lamb.

When he reached the yard in front of the house he threw him roughly on the ground and, putting his foot on his neck, he said to him: "It is late, and I want to go to bed; we will settle our accounts tomorrow. In the meanwhile, as the dog who kept guard at night died today, you shall take his place at once. You shall be my watchdog."

Taking a great collar covered with brass knobs, the farmer strapped it tightly round Pinocchio's throat so that he might not be able to draw his head out of it. A heavy chain attached to the collar was fastened to the wall.

"If it should rain tonight," the farmer then said to Pinocchio, "you can go and lie down in the kennel. The straw that has served as a bed for my poor dog for the last four years is still there. If unfortunately robbers should come, remember to keep your ears pricked and to bark."

After giving him this last order the man went into the house, shut the door and drew the chain across.

Pinocchio

Poor Pinocchio remained lying on the ground, more dead than alive from the effects of cold, hunger, and fear. From time to time he put his hands angrily to the collar that tightened his throat and said, crying: "It serves me right! I was determined to be a layabout and I listened to bad companions. If I had been a good little boy, as so many are; if I had been willing to learn and to work; if I had remained at home with my poor papa, I should not now be in the midst of the fields and obliged to be the watchdog outside a farmer's house. But now it is too late and I must have patience!"

Relieved by this little outburst, which came straight from his heart, he went into the dog-kennel and fell asleep.

Chapter 21

Pinocchio discovers the robbers and, as a
reward for his loyalty, is set free.

PINOCCHIO had been sleeping heavily for about two hours
when, towards midnight, he was roused by a whispering of
strange voices that seemed to come from the courtyard.
Putting the point of his nose out of the kennel, he saw four little
beasts with dark fur standing together. They looked like cats – but
they were not cats; they were polecats: carnivorous little animals,
especially greedy for eggs and young chickens. One of the polecats,
leaving his companions, came to the opening of the kennel and said in
a low voice: "Good evening, Melampo."

"My name is not Melampo," answered the puppet.

"Oh! Then where is Melampo? Where is the old dog who lived in
this kennel?"

"He died this morning."

"Is he dead? Poor beast! He was so good. But judging you by your
face I should say that you are also a good dog."

"I beg your pardon, I am not a dog."

"Not a dog? Then what are you?"

"I am a puppet."

"And you are acting as watchdog?"

"Yes, that's right – as a punishment."

"Well, then, I will offer you the same conditions that we made with
the deceased Melampo, and I am sure you will be satisfied with them."

"What are these conditions?"

"One night in every week you are to permit us to visit this poultry-yard as we have hitherto done, and to carry off eight chickens. Of these chickens, seven are to be eaten by us and one we will give to you, on the express understanding, however, that you pretend to be asleep, and that it never enters your head to bark and to wake the farmer."

"Did Melampo do that?" asked Pinocchio.

"Certainly, and we were always on the best terms with him. Sleep quietly and rest assured that before we go we will leave by the kennel a beautiful chicken ready plucked for your breakfast tomorrow. Have we understood each other clearly?"

"Only too clearly!" answered Pinocchio, and he shook his head threateningly as much as to say: 'You shall hear of this shortly!'

The four polecats, thinking themselves safe, slunk over to the poultry-yard, which was close to the kennel. They opened the wooden gate with their teeth and claws, and slipped in one by one. But they had only just passed through when they heard the gate shut behind them with a great slam.

It was Pinocchio who had shut it; and for greater security he put a large stone against it to keep it closed. He then began to bark, and he barked exactly like a watchdog: "Bow-wow! Bow-wow!"

Hearing the barking, the farmer jumped out of bed and, taking his gun, he came to the window and asked: "What is the matter?"

"There are robbers!" answered Pinocchio.

The farmer was there in less time than it takes to say 'Amen'. He rushed into the poultry-yard, caught the polecats and, put them into a sack.

He then approached Pinocchio and began to pet him. Amongst other things he asked him: "How did you manage to discover the four thieves? To think my faithful Melampo, never found out anything!"

Chapter 21

The puppet might then have told him the whole story. He might have informed him of the disgraceful conditions that had been made between the dog and the polecats. But he remembered that the dog was dead, and he thought to himself: 'What is the good of accusing the dead? The dead are dead, and the best thing to be done is to leave them in peace!'

"As a proof of my gratitude," cried the farmer, clapping Pinocchio on the shoulder, "I will at once set you free. You may return home."

And he removed the dog collar.

Chapter 22

Pinocchio mourns the death of the beautiful child with the blue hair. He then meets with a Pigeon who flies with him to the seashore. There he throws himself into the water to go to the assistance of his father, Geppetto.

As soon as Pinocchio was released from the heavy and humiliating weight of the dog collar, he started off across the fields and never stopped until he had reached the high road that led to the Fairy's house. There, he turned and looked down into the plain beneath. He could see distinctly with his naked eye the wood where he had been so unfortunate as to meet with the Fox and the Cat. He could see amongst the trees the top of the Big Oak to which he had been hanged. But although he looked in every direction, the little house belonging to the beautiful child with the blue hair was nowhere visible.

Seized with dread, he began to run with all the strength he had left, and in a few minutes he reached the field where the little white house had once stood. But the little white house was no longer there. He saw instead a marble stone, on which were engraved these sad words:

HERE LIES
THE CHILD WITH THE BLUE HAIR
WHO DIED FROM SORROW
BECAUSE SHE WAS ABANDONED BY HER
LITTLE BROTHER PINOCCHIO.

Chapter 22

The puppet fell with his face on the ground and, covering the tombstone with a thousand kisses, burst into an agony of tears. He cried all night, and when morning came he was still crying – although he had no tears left. His sobs and lamentations were so acute and heartbreaking that they roused the echoes in the surrounding hills.

In his despair he tried to tear his hair; but as his hair was made of wood, he did not have the satisfaction of sticking his fingers into it.

Just then a large Pigeon flew over his head and, pausing with its wings outstretched, called down to him from a great height: "Tell me, child, what are you doing there?"

"Don't you see? I am crying!" said Pinocchio, raising his head towards the voice and rubbing his eyes with his jacket.

"Tell me," continued the Pigeon, "amongst your companions, do you happen to know a puppet who is called Pinocchio?"

"Pinocchio? Did you say Pinocchio?" repeated the puppet, jumping to his feet. "I am Pinocchio!"

At this answer, the Pigeon descended rapidly to the ground. He was larger than a turkey. "Do you also know Geppetto?" he asked.

"Do I know him! He is my poor papa! Has he perhaps spoken to you of me? Will you take me to him? Is he still alive? Answer me, for pity's sake: is he still alive?"

"I left him three days ago on the seashore."

"What was he doing?"

"He was building a little boat for himself, to cross the ocean. For more than three months that poor man has been going in all directions looking for you. Not having succeeded in finding you, he has now taken it into his head to go to the distant countries of the new world in search of you."

"How far is it from here to the shore?" asked Pinocchio breathlessly.

"More than six hundred miles."

Pinocchio

"Six hundred miles! Oh, beautiful Pigeon, what a fine thing it would be to have your wings!"

"If you wish to go, I will carry you there."

"How?"

"Astride my back. Do you weigh much?"

"I weigh next to nothing. I am as light as a feather."

And, without waiting for more, Pinocchio jumped at once on the Pigeon's back. Putting a leg on each side of him, as men do on horseback, he exclaimed joyfully: "Gallop, gallop, my little horse, for I am anxious to arrive quickly!"

The Pigeon took flight, and in a few minutes had soared so high that they almost touched the clouds. Finding himself at such an immense height, the puppet had the curiosity to turn and look down. But his head spun round and he became so frightened that, to save himself from the danger of falling, he wound his arms tightly round the neck of his feathered steed.

They flew all day and night, and the following morning they reached the seashore. The Pigeon placed Pinocchio on the ground and, not wishing to be troubled with thanks for having done a good turn, flew quickly away and disappeared.

The shore was crowded with people who were looking out to sea, shouting and gesticulating.

"What has happened?" asked Pinocchio of an old woman.

"A poor father who has lost his son has gone away in a boat to search for him on the other side of the water, and today the sea is tempestuous and the little boat is in danger of sinking."

"Where is the little boat?"

"It is out there in a line with my finger," said the old woman, pointing to a little boat which, seen at that distance, looked like a nutshell with a very little man in it.

Pinocchio fixed his eyes on it and, after looking attentively, he gave

a piercing scream, crying: "It is my papa! It is my papa!"

The boat meanwhile, beaten by the fury of the waves, at one moment disappeared in the trough of the sea, and the next came again to the surface. Pinocchio, standing on the top of a high rock, kept calling to his father by name, and making every kind of signal to him with his hands, his handkerchief, and his cap.

And although he was so far off, Geppetto appeared to recognise his son, for he also took off his cap and waved it, and tried by gestures to make him understand that he would have returned if it had been possible, but that the sea was so tempestuous that he could not use his oars or approach the shore.

Suddenly a tremendous wave rose and the boat disappeared. They waited, hoping it would come again to the surface, but it was seen no more.

"Poor man!" said the fishermen who were assembled on the shore and, murmuring a prayer, they turned to go home.

But just then they heard a desperate cry and, looking back, they saw a little boy who exclaimed, as he jumped from a rock into the sea: "I will save my papa!"

Pinocchio, being made of wood, floated easily and he swam like a fish. At one moment they saw him disappear under the water, carried down by the fury of the waves. The next he reappeared, struggling with a leg or an arm. But at last they lost sight of him and he was seen no more.

"Poor boy!" said the fishermen who were collected on the shore and, once again murmuring a prayer, they returned home.

Chapter 23

Pinocchio arrives at the Island of the
Busy Bees and finds the Fairy again.

PINOCCHIO, hoping to be in time to help his father, swam the
whole night. And what a horrible night it was! The rain came
down in torrents; it hailed; the thunder was frightful; and the
flashes of lightning made it as light as day.

Towards morning, Pinocchio saw a long strip of land not far off. It
was an island in the midst of the sea. He tried his utmost to reach the
shore: but it was all in vain. The waves racing and tumbling over each
other knocked him about as if he had been a stick or a wisp of straw.
At last, fortunately for him, a billow rolled up with such fury and
force that he was lifted up and thrown violently far on to the sands.
He fell with such force that, as he struck the ground, his ribs and all
his joints cracked. But he comforted himself saying: "And again I have
made a wonderful escape!"

Little by little the sky cleared, the sun shone out in all his
splendour, and the sea became as quiet and smooth as oil.

The puppet put his clothes in the sun to dry, and began to look in
every direction in the hope of seeing on the vast expanse of water a
little boat with a man in it. But although he looked and looked, he
could see nothing but the sky and the sea – and the sail of some ship,
but so far away that it seemed no bigger than a fly.

"If I only knew what this island was called!" Pinocchio said to
himself. "If I only knew whether it was inhabited by civilised people

Pinocchio

– I mean by people who have not got the bad habit of hanging boys to the branches of the trees. But who can I ask? Who, if there is nobody?"

This idea of finding himself alone, alone, all alone, in the midst of this great uninhabited country, made him so melancholy that he was just beginning to cry. But at that moment, at a short distance from the shore, he saw a big fish swimming by; it was going quietly on its own business with its head out of the water.

Not knowing its name, the puppet called to it in a loud voice to make himself heard: "Hey, Sir Fish, will you allow me a word with you?"

"Two if you like," answered the fish, who was a Dolphin – and so polite that few similar are to be found in any sea in the world.

"Will you be kind enough to tell me if there are villages in this island where it would be possible to obtain something to eat, without running the danger of being eaten?"

"Certainly there are," replied the Dolphin. "Indeed you will find one at a short distance from here."

"And what road must I take to go there?"

"You must take that path to your left and follow your nose. You cannot make a mistake."

"Will you tell me another thing? You who swim about the sea all day and all night, have you by chance met a little boat with my papa in it?"

"And who is your papa?"

"He is the best papa in the world, whilst it would be difficult to find a worse son than I am."

"During the terrible storm last night," answered the Dolphin, "the little boat must have gone to the bottom."

"And my papa?"

"He must have been swallowed by the terrible Dogfish shark who for some days past has been spreading terror and panic in our waters."

"Is this Dogfish shark very big?" asked Pinocchio, who was already beginning to quake with fear.

"Big?" replied the Dolphin. "So that you may form some idea of his size, I need only tell you that he is bigger than a five-storey house, and that his mouth is so enormous and so deep that a railway train with its smoking engine could pass easily down his throat."

"Mercy upon us!" exclaimed the terrified puppet. Putting on his clothes with the greatest haste, he said to the Dolphin: "Goodbye, Sir Fish. Excuse the trouble I have given you – and many thanks for your politeness."

He then took the path that had been pointed out to him and began to walk fast – so fast, indeed, that he was almost running. And at the slightest noise he turned to look behind him, fearing that he might see the terrible Dogfish shark with a railway train in its mouth, following him.

After a walk of half an hour he reached a little village called the Village of the Busy Bees. The road was alive with people running here and there to attend to their business: all were at work, all had something to do. You could not have found an idler nor a layabout even if you had searched for him with a lighted lamp.

"Ah!" said that lazy Pinocchio at once, "I see that this village will never suit me! I wasn't born to work!"

In the meanwhile he was tormented by hunger. What was he to do?

At that moment a man came down the road, tired and panting for breath. He was dragging alone, with fatigue and difficulty, two carts full of charcoal.

Pinocchio, judging by his face that he was a kind man, approached him and, casting down his eyes with shame, he said to him in a low voice: "Would you have the charity to give me a halfpenny, for I am dying of hunger?"

"You shall have not only a halfpenny," said the man, "but I will give you twopence, provided that you help me to drag home these two carts of charcoal."

"I am surprised at you!" answered the puppet in a tone of offence. "Let me tell you that I am not accustomed to do the work of a donkey: I have never drawn a cart!"

"You are lucky then," answered the man. "So my boy, if you are really dying of hunger, eat two fine slices of your pride and be careful not to get an indigestion."

In less than half an hour twenty other people went by. Pinocchio asked charity of them all, but they all answered: "Are you not ashamed to beg? Instead of idling about the roads, go and look for a little work and learn to earn your bread."

At last a nice little woman carrying two cans of water came by.

"Will you let me drink a little water out of your can?" asked Pinocchio, who was burning with thirst.

"Drink, my boy, if you wish it!" said the little woman, setting down the two cans.

Pinocchio drank like a fish and, as he dried his mouth, he mumbled: "I have quenched my thirst. If I could only appease my hunger!"

The good woman, hearing these words, said at once: "If you will help me to carry home these two cans of water, I will give you a fine piece of bread. And besides the bread you shall have a nice dish of cauliflower dressed with oil and vinegar," added the good woman. "And after the cauliflower I will give you a beautiful cake with syrup."

The temptation of this last dainty was so great that Pinocchio could resist no longer and said firmly: "I must have patience! I will carry the can to your house."

The can was heavy and the puppet, not being strong enough to

carry it in his hand, had to resign himself to carry it on his head.

When they reached the house, the good little woman made Pinocchio sit down at a small table already laid, and she placed before him the bread, the cauliflower, and the cake.

Pinocchio did not eat the food, he devoured it. His stomach was like an apartment that had been left empty and uninhabited for five months.

When his ravenous hunger was somewhat eased he raised his head to thank his benefactress. But he had no sooner looked at her than he gave a long "Oh-h-h!" of astonishment. He stared at her with wide-open eyes, his fork in the air, and his mouth full of bread and cauliflower, as if he had been bewitched.

"What has surprised you so much?" asked the good woman, laughing.

"It is... " answered the puppet, "it is... it is... that you are like... that you remind me... yes, yes, yes, the same voice... the same eyes... the same hair... yes, yes, yes... you also have blue hair, as she had... Oh, little Fairy! Tell me that it is you, really you! Do not make me cry any more! If you knew...! I have cried so much, I have suffered so much!"

And, throwing himself at her feet on the floor, Pinocchio embraced the knees of the mysterious little woman and began to cry bitterly.

Chapter 24

Pinocchio promises the Fairy to be good and studious, for he is quite sick of being a puppet and wishes to become a real boy.

AT first the good little woman maintained that she was not the little Fairy with blue hair. But then, seeing that she was found out, and not wishing to continue the jest any longer, she ended by making herself known. She said to Pinocchio: "Do you remember? You left me a child, and now that you have found me again I am a woman – a woman almost old enough to be your mother."

"I am delighted at that, for now, instead of calling you little sister, I will call you mamma. I have wished for such a long time to have a mother like other boys! But how did you manage to grow so fast?"

"That is a secret."

"Teach it to me, for I should also like to grow. Don't you see? I always remain no bigger than a ninepin."

"But you cannot grow," replied the Fairy.

"Why?"

"Because puppets never grow. They are born puppets, live puppets, and die puppets."

"Oh, I am sick of being a puppet!" cried Pinocchio, giving himself a slap. "It is time that I became a man..."

"And you will become one, if you know how to deserve it..."

"Really? And what can I do to deserve it?"

"A very easy thing: by learning to be a good boy."

Pinocchio

"And you think I am not?"

"You are quite the contrary. Good boys are obedient, and you..."

"And I never obey."

"Good boys like to learn and to work, and you..."

"And I instead lead an idle layabout life the whole year through."

"Good boys always speak the truth..."

"And I always tell lies."

"Good boys go willingly to school..."

"And school makes me feel ill. But from today I will change my life."

"Do you promise me?"

"I promise you. I will become a good little boy and I will be the comfort of my papa – where is my poor papa at this moment? Shall I ever have the happiness of seeing him again and kissing him?"

"I think so; indeed I am sure of it."

At this answer Pinocchio was so delighted that he took the Fairy's hands and began to kiss them with joy, quite beside himself. Then, raising his face and looking at her lovingly, he asked: "Tell me, little mamma: then it was not true that you were dead?"

"It seems not," said the Fairy, smiling.

"If you only knew the sorrow I felt and the tightening of my throat when I read, 'here lies...'"

"I know it, and it is on that account that I have forgiven you. I saw from the sincerity of your grief that you had a good heart.

And when boys have good hearts, even if they are scamps and have got bad habits, there is always something to hope for – that is, there is always hope that they will turn to better ways. That is why I came to look for you here. I will be your mamma…"

"Oh, how delightful!" shouted Pinocchio, jumping for joy.

"You must obey me and do everything that I bid you."

"Willingly, willingly, willingly!"

"Tomorrow," announced the Fairy, "you will begin to go to school. Then you must choose a skill, or a trade, whatever you wish."

Lifting his head quickly, Pinocchio said to the Fairy: "I will study, I will work, I will do all that you tell me. For indeed I have become weary of being a puppet and I wish at any price to become a boy. You promised me that I should, did you not?"

"I did promise you – and it now depends upon yourself."

Chapter 25

Pinocchio accompanies his school fellows to the seashore to see the terrible Dogfish shark.

THE following day Pinocchio went to the local school.
Imagine the delight of all the little pupils when they saw a puppet walk into their classroom! They sent up a roar of laughter that never seemed to end.

They played all sorts of tricks on him. One boy carried off his cap. Another pulled the back of his jacket. One tried to draw an inky moustache just under his nose. And another attempted to tie strings to his feet and hands to make him dance.

For a short time Pinocchio pretended not to care and got on as well as he could; but at last losing all patience, he turned to those who were teasing him most and making fun of him, and said to them, looking very angry: "Beware, boys. I have not come here to be your clown. I'll respect you and I expect you to respect me."

"Well said, egg-head! You have spoken like a book!" howled the boys, convulsed with mad laughter. And one of them, even bolder than the others, stretched out his hand intending to seize the puppet by the end of his nose.

But he was not in time, for Pinocchio stuck his leg out from under the table and gave him a great kick on his shins.

"Oh, what hard feet!" roared the boy, rubbing the bruise that the puppet had given him.

"And what elbows – even harder than his feet!" said another, who received a blow from Pinocchio in the stomach because of his unkind tricks.

But nevertheless the kick and the blow at once won for Pinocchio the sympathy and the esteem of all the boys in the school. They all made friends with him and liked him heartily.

Even the teacher praised Pinocchio, for he found him attentive, studious, and intelligent – he was always the first to come to school, and the last to leave when school was over.

However, Pinocchio had one fault: he made too many friends – and amongst them were several young rascals well known for their dislike of study and love of mischief.

The teacher warned him every day, and even the good Fairy never failed to tell him, and to repeat constantly: "Take care, Pinocchio! Those bad school fellows of yours will end sooner or later by making you lose all your love of study. Perhaps they may even bring upon you some great misfortune."

"Have no fear of that!" answered the puppet, shrugging his shoulders and touching his forehead as much as to say: "There is too much sense here for that!"

Now it happened that one fine day, as he was on his way to school, he met several of his usual companions who, coming up to him, asked: "Have you heard the great news?"

"No."

"In the sea near here a Dogfish shark has appeared, as big as a mountain."

"Not really? Can it be the same Dogfish shark that was there when my poor papa was drowned?"

"We are going to the shore to see him. Will you come with us?"

"No; I am going to school."

"What does school matter? We can go to school tomorrow. Whether we have a lesson more or a lesson less, we shall always remain the same donkeys."

"But what will the teacher say?"

"The teacher may say what he likes. He is paid specifically to grumble all day."

"And my mamma?"

"Mammas know nothing," answered those bad little boys.

"Do you know what I will do?" said Pinocchio. "I have reasons for wishing to see the Dogfish shark, but I will go and see him when school is over."

"Poor little donkey!" exclaimed one of the number. "Do you suppose that a fish of that size will wait at your convenience? As soon as he is tired of being here he will set out for another place, and then it will be too late."

"How long does it take from here to the shore?" asked the puppet.

"We can be there and back in an hour."

"Then away!" shouted Pinocchio. "And he who runs fastest is the best!"

Chapter 26

A great fight between Pinocchio and his companions. One of them is wounded and Pinocchio is arrested by the officers.

WHEN he arrived on the shore, Pinocchio looked out to sea; but he saw no Dogfish shark. The sea was as smooth as a great crystal mirror.

"Where is the Dogfish shark?" he asked, turning to his companions.

"He must have gone to have his breakfast," said one of them, laughing.

"Or he has thrown himself on to his bed to have a little nap," added another, laughing still louder.

From their absurd answers and silly laughter Pinocchio realised that his companions had been making a fool of him, encouraging him to believe a tale with no truth in it. Taking it very badly, he said to them angrily: "And now may I ask how much fun you have had in deceiving me with the story of the Dogfish?"

"Oh, it was great fun!" answered the little rascals in chorus.

"And why exactly did you find it fun?"

"In making you miss school, and persuading you to come with us. Are you not embarrassed of always being on time and paying such attention to your lessons? Are you not embarrassed of studying so hard?"

"And if I study hard, what concern is it of yours?"

"It's of great concern, because it makes us look bad before the teacher."

Pinocchio

"Really," said the puppet, shaking his head, "you make me want to laugh."

"Hey, Pinocchio!" shouted the biggest of the boys, confronting him. "Enough of your superior airs! Don't come here to crow over us! You may not be afraid of us, but we are not afraid of you. Remember that you are just one against seven of us."

"Seven, like the seven deadly sins," said Pinocchio with a shout.

"Listen! He has insulted us all! He called us the seven deadly sins!"

"Pinocchio! Beg us to forgive you – or you'll be sorry!"

"Cuckoo!" sang the puppet, putting his thumb at the end of his nose and wiggling his fingers scoffingly.

"Pinocchio! It will end badly!"

"Cuckoo!"

"We'll beat you like a donkey!"

"Cuckoo!"

"You will return home with a broken nose!"

"Cuckoo!"

"I'll give you cuckoo!" said the most courageous of the boys. "Take that to begin with – and keep it for your supper tonight." And so saying, he gave him a blow on the head with his fist.

But it was give and take; for the puppet, as was to be expected, immediately returned the blow. In a moment, everyone was fighting.

Pinocchio, although he was one alone, defended himself like a hero. He used his feet, which were of the hardest wood, to such purpose that he kept his enemies at a respectful distance. Wherever they touched they left a bruise by way of reminder.

The boys, becoming furious at not being able to measure themselves hand to hand with the puppet, turned to other weapons. Loosening their satchels, they commenced throwing their schoolbooks at him: grammar books, dictionaries, ABC books, geography books, and other textbooks. But Pinocchio was quick and had sharp eyes, and

always managed to duck in time, so that the books passed over his head and all fell into the sea.

Imagine the astonishment of the fish! Thinking that the books were something to eat, they all arrived in shoals. But, having tasted a page or two, or a frontispiece, they spat them quickly out and made wry faces that seemed to say: 'It isn't food for us; we are accustomed to something much better!'

The battle meantime had become fiercer than ever, when a big crab, who had come out of the water and had climbed slowly up on to the shore, called out in a hoarse voice that sounded like a trumpet with a bad cold: "Have done, you young ruffians! For that's what you surely are! These hand-to-hand fights between boys seldom finish well. Some disaster is sure to happen!"

The poor crab! He might as well have preached to the wind.

Just then, the boys, who had no more books of their own to throw, spied at a little distance the satchel that belonged to Pinocchio. They grabbed it in less time than it takes to tell.

Amongst the books there was one bound in strong cardboard and parchment. It was a Treatise on Arithmetic. I leave you to imagine if it was big or not!

One of the boys seized this volume and, aiming at Pinocchio's head, threw it at him with all the force he could muster. But instead of hitting the puppet, it struck one of his companions on the temple, who, turning as white as a sheet, said only: "Oh, Mother, help – I am dying!" and fell headlong onto the sand. Thinking he was dead, the terrified boys ran off as hard as their legs could carry them, and in a few minutes they were out of sight.

But Pinocchio remained. He ran and soaked his handkerchief in the sea and began to bathe the temples of his poor school fellow, Eugene. Crying bitterly in his despair he began to strike his head with his fists, and to call poor Eugene by his name.

Chapter 26

Suddenly he heard the sound of approaching footsteps. He turned and saw two cavalry soldiers.

"What are you doing there, lying on the ground?" they asked Pinocchio.

"I am helping my school fellow.

"Has he been hurt?"

"So it seems."

"Hurt indeed!" said one of the soldiers, stooping down and examining Eugene closely. "This boy has been wounded in the temple. Who wounded him?"

"Not I," stammered the puppet breathlessly.

"If it was not you, who then did it?

"Not I," repeated Pinocchio.

"And with what was he wounded?"

"With this book." And the puppet picked up from the ground the Treatise on Arithmetic, bound in cardboard and parchment, and showed it to the soldier.

"And to whom does this book belong?"

"To me."

"That is enough: nothing more is wanted. Get up and come with us at once."

"But I—"

"Come along with us!"

"But I am innocent..."

"Come along with us!"

Before they left, the soldiers called some fishermen, who were passing at that moment near the shore in their boat, and said to them: "We give this boy who has been wounded in the head into your charge. Carry him to your house and nurse him. Tomorrow we will come and see him."

They then turned to Pinocchio and, having placed him between them, they said to him in a commanding voice: "Forward! And walk quickly! Or it will be the worse for you."

Without needing it to be repeated, the puppet set out along the road leading to the village. But the poor little devil hardly knew where he was. He thought he must be dreaming – and what a dreadful dream! He was beside himself. He saw double; his legs shook; his tongue clung to the roof of his mouth, and he could not utter a word. And yet in the midst of his daze and dismay, his heart was pierced by a cruel thorn – the thought that he would have to pass under the windows of the good Fairy's house between the soldiers. He would rather have died.

They had already reached the village when a gust of wind blew Pinocchio's cap off his head and carried it ten yards off.

"Will you permit me," said the puppet to the soldiers, "to go and get my cap?"

"Go, then; but be quick about it."

The puppet went and picked up his cap – but instead of putting it on his head, he took it between his teeth and began to run as hard as he could towards the seashore.

The soldiers, thinking it would be difficult to overtake him, sent after him a large mastiff who had won the first prizes at all the dog races. Pinocchio ran, but the dog ran faster. The people came to their windows and crowded into the street in their anxiety to see the end of the desperate race. But they could not satisfy their curiosity, for Pinocchio and the dog raised such clouds of dust that in a few minutes nothing could be seen of either of them.

Chapter 27

Pinocchio is in danger of being fried
in a frying-pan like a fish.

THERE came a moment in this desperate race – a terrible moment – when Pinocchio thought himself lost. For you must know that Alidoro – for so the mastiff was called – had run so swiftly that he had nearly caught up with him.

The puppet could hear the panting of the dreadful beast close behind him; there was not a hand's breadth between them – he could even feel the dog's hot breath.

Fortunately the shore was close and the sea but a few steps off.

As soon as he reached the sands, the puppet made a wonderful leap – a frog could have done no better – and plunged into the water.

Alidoro, on the contrary, wished to stop himself but, carried away by the momentum of the race, he also went into the sea. The unfortunate dog could not swim. He made great efforts to keep himself afloat with his paws, but the more he struggled the farther he sank head downwards under the water.

When he rose once to the surface, his eyes rolled with terror, and he barked out: "I am drowning! Help me, dear Pinocchio! Save me from death!"

At that agonising cry, the puppet was moved with compassion. Turning to the dog he said: "If I save your life, will you promise to annoy me no further and not to run after me?"

"I promise! I promise! Be quick, for pity's sake, for if you delay another half-minute I shall be dead."

Pinocchio swam to Alidoro and, taking hold of his tail with both hands, brought him safe and sound on to the dry sand of the beach.

The poor dog could not stand. He had drunk, against his will, so much saltwater that he was like a balloon. The puppet, however, not wishing to trust him too far, thought it more prudent to jump again into the water. When he had swum some distance from the shore he called out to the friend he had rescued: "Goodbye, Alidoro. A good journey to you, and take my compliments to all at home."

"Goodbye, Pinocchio," answered the dog. "A thousand thanks for having saved my life. You have done me a great service – and in this world what is given is returned. If an occasion offers itself, I shall not forget it."

Pinocchio swam on, keeping always near the land. At last he thought that he had reached a safe place. Giving a look along the shore he saw amongst the rocks a kind of cave from which a cloud of smoke was ascending.

"So," he said to himself, "there must be a fire. So much the better. I will go and dry and warm myself – and then? And then we shall see."

Having taken this resolution he approached the rocks; but as he was going to climb up, he felt something under the water that rose higher and higher and carried him into the air. He tried to escape, but it was too late, for to his extreme surprise he found himself enclosed in a great net, together with a swarm of fish of every size and shape, who were flapping and struggling like so many despairing souls.

At the same moment a fisherman came out of the cave. He was so ugly, so horribly ugly, that he looked like a sea-monster. Instead of hair his head was covered with a thick bush of green grass; his skin was green; his eyes were green; his long beard that came down to the ground was also green. He had the appearance of an immense lizard standing on its hind paws.

Chapter 27

When the fisherman had drawn his net out of the sea, he exclaimed with great satisfaction: "Thank Heaven! Again today I shall have a splendid feast of fish!"

"What a mercy that I am not a fish!" said Pinocchio to himself, regaining a little courage.

The net full of fish was carried into the cave, which was dark and smoky. In the middle of the cave a large frying-pan full of oil was frying, and sending out a smell of mushrooms that was suffocating.

"Now we will see what fish we have taken!" said the green fisherman. Putting into the net an enormous hand, so out of all proportion that it looked like a baker's shovel, he pulled out a handful of mullet.

"These mullet are good!" he said, looking at them and smelling them complacently. And after he had smelt them he threw them into a pan without water.

He repeated the same operation many times; and as he drew out the fish, his mouth watered and he said, chuckling to himself: "What good whiting!"

"What exquisite sardines!"

"These soles are delicious!"

"And these crabs excellent!"

"What dear little anchovies!"

I need not tell you that the whiting, the sardines, the soles, the crabs, and the anchovies were all thrown into the pan to keep company with the mullet.

The last to remain in the net was Pinocchio.

No sooner had the fisherman taken him out than he opened his big green eyes with astonishment and cried, half-frightened: "What species of fish is this? I don't remember ever eating any fish of this kind!"

The green fisherman looked at Pinocchio again attentively and, having examined him well all over, he ended by saying: "I know: he must be a lobster."

Pinocchio, mortified at being mistaken for a lobster, said in an angry voice: "A lobster indeed! Do you take me for a lobster? How dare you! Let me tell you that I am a puppet."

"A puppet?" replied the fisherman. "To tell the truth, a puppet is quite a new fish for me. All the better! I shall eat you with greater pleasure."

"Eat me? But do you understand that I am not a fish? Don't you hear that I talk and reason as you do?"

"That is quite true," said the fisherman; "and as I see that you are a fish possessed of the talent of talking and reasoning as I do, I will leave you the choice of how you would like to be cooked. Would you like to be fried in the frying-pan, or would you prefer to be stewed with tomato sauce?"

"To tell the truth," answered Pinocchio, "if I am to choose, I should prefer to be set at liberty and to return home."

"You are joking! Do you imagine that I would lose the opportunity of tasting such a rare fish? It is not every day, I assure you, that a puppet fish is caught in these waters. Leave it to me. I will fry you in the frying-pan with the other fish, and you will be quite satisfied. It is always a comfort to be fried in company."

At this speech, the unhappy Pinocchio began to cry and scream and to implore for mercy, and he wriggled like an eel, and made indescribable efforts to slip out of the clutches of the green fisherman.

But it was useless: the fisherman took a long strip of rush and, having bound his hands and feet as if he had been a sausage, he threw him into the pan with the other fish.

He then fetched a wooden bowl full of flour and began to flour them each in turn, and as soon as they were ready he threw them into the frying-pan.

Pinocchio

The first to dance in the boiling oil were the poor whiting; the crabs followed, then the sardines, then the soles, then the anchovies, and at last it was Pinocchio's turn. Seeing himself so near death – and such a horrible death – he was so frightened, and trembled so violently, that he had neither voice nor breath left for further pleading.

The poor boy implored with his eyes. But the green fisherman, however, without caring in the least, plunged him five or six times in the flour, until he was white from head to foot, and looked like a puppet made of plaster.

He then took him by the head, and...

Chapter 28

Pinocchio returns to the Fairy's house. She promises him that the following day he shall cease to be a puppet and shall become a boy. There will be a grand breakfast of coffee and milk to celebrate this great event.

JUST as the fisherman was on the point of throwing Pinocchio into the frying-pan, a large dog entered the cave, enticed there by the strong and savoury odour of fried fish.

"Get out!" shouted the fisherman threateningly, holding the floured puppet in his hand, and he stretched out his leg to give him a kick.

But the dog turned upon him, growling and showing his terrible fangs. He made a spring, seized the bundle in his mouth and, holding it gently between his teeth, he rushed out of the cave and was gone like a flash of lightning.

When Alidoro had reached the path that led to the village, he stopped and put his friend Pinocchio gently on the ground.

"How much I have to thank you for!" said the puppet.

"There is no need," replied the dog. "You saved me and I have now returned the favour. You know that we must all help each other in this world."

Alidoro extended his right paw to the puppet, who shook it heartily in token of great friendship, and they then separated. The dog took the road home and Pinocchio set off for the village.

But as he went, he felt very uneasy – so dismayed, indeed, that for every two steps forwards he took another backwards. He talked to himself as he went, saying: "How shall I ever present myself to my good little Fairy? What will she say when she sees me? Oh, I am sure that she will not forgive me! And it serves me right, for I am a rascal. I am always promising to correct myself, and I never keep my word!"

When he reached the village it was night and very dark. A storm had come on and, as the rain was coming down in torrents he went straight to the Fairy's house, resolving to knock at the door and hoping to be let in.

But when he was there his courage failed him, and instead of knocking he ran away some twenty paces. He returned to the door a second time, but could not make up his mind. He came back a third time – still he dared not. The fourth time, he laid hold of the knocker and, trembling, gave a little knock.

He waited and waited. At last, after half an hour had passed, a window on the top floor was opened – the house was four storeys high – and Pinocchio saw a big Snail with a lighted candle on her head looking out. She called to him: "Who is there at this hour?"

"Is the Fairy at home?" asked the puppet.

"The Fairy is asleep and must not be wakened. But who are you?"

"It is I!"

"Who is I?"

"Pinocchio."

"And who is Pinocchio?"

"The puppet who lives in the Fairy's house."

"Ah, I understand!" said the Snail. "Wait for me there. I will come down and open the door straight away."

"Be quick, for pity's sake, for I am dying of cold."

"My boy, I am a snail, and snails are never in a hurry."

An hour passed, and then two, and the door was not opened. Pinocchio, who was wet through, and trembling from cold and fear, at last took courage and knocked again – and this time he knocked louder.

Pinocchio

At this second knock, a window on the lower storey opened and the same Snail appeared at it.

"Beautiful little Snail," cried Pinocchio from the street, "I have been waiting for two hours! And two hours on such a bad night seem longer than two years. Be quick, for pity's sake."

"My boy," answered the calm, unruffled little animal, "my boy, I am a snail, and snails are never in a hurry."

And the window was shut again.

Shortly afterwards midnight struck; then one o'clock, then two o'clock, and the door remained still closed.

Pinocchio, at last losing all patience, seized the knocker in a rage, intending to give a blow that would resound through the house. But the knocker, which was iron, turned suddenly into an eel, and slipping out of his hands disappeared in the stream of water that ran down the middle of the street.

"Ah! Is that it?" shouted Pinocchio, blind with rage. "Since the knocker has disappeared, I will instead kick with all my might." And drawing a little back, he gave a tremendous kick against the house door. The blow was indeed so forceful that his foot went through the wood and stuck! He tried to draw it back again, but it was no use. It remained fixed there like a nail that has been hammered down.

Think of poor Pinocchio! He was obliged to spend the remainder of the night with one foot on the ground and the other in the air.

The following morning at daybreak the door was at last opened. That brave little Snail had taken only nine hours to come down from the fourth storey to the house door. She must have put all her efforts into it.

"What are you doing with your foot stuck in the door?" she asked the puppet, laughing.

"It was an accident. Do try, beautiful little Snail, to see if you can release me from this torture."

"My boy, that is the work of a carpenter, and I have never been a carpenter."

"Then beg the Fairy for me!"

"The Fairy is asleep and must not be wakened."

"But what do you suppose that I can do all day, nailed to this door?"

"Amuse yourself by counting the ants that pass down the street."

"Bring me at least something to eat, for I am quite exhausted."

"At once," said the Snail.

In fact, after three and a half hours she returned to Pinocchio carrying a silver tray on her head. The tray contained a loaf of bread, a roast chicken, and four ripe apricots.

"Here is the breakfast that the Fairy has sent you," said the Snail.

The puppet felt very much comforted at the sight of these good things. But when he began to eat them, he found to his disgust that the bread was plaster, the chicken cardboard, and the four apricots painted alabaster!

He wanted to cry. In his desperation, he tried to throw away the tray and all that was on it; but instead, either from grief or exhaustion, he fainted away.

When he came to, he found that he was lying on a sofa, and the Fairy was beside him.

"I will pardon you once more," the Fairy said, "but woe to you if you behave badly a third time!"

Pinocchio promised, and swore that he would study and in future always conduct himself well.

And he kept his word for the remainder of the year.

Indeed, when it finally came to the examinations before the holidays, he had the honour of being the first in the school! His behaviour in general was so good and praiseworthy that the Fairy was very pleased, and said to him: "Tomorrow your wish shall be granted."

"And that is?"

"Tomorrow you shall cease to be a wooden puppet and you shall become a boy."

You could not imagine Pinocchio's joy at this longed-for good fortune if you did not see it yourself. All his school fellows were to be invited for the following day to a grand breakfast at the Fairy's house, so that they might celebrate the great event together. The Fairy had prepared two hundred cups of coffee with milk, and four hundred rolls cut and buttered on each side. The day promised to be most happy and delightful, but...

Unfortunately, in the lives of puppets there is always a 'but' that spoils everything.

Chapter 29

Pinocchio, instead of becoming a boy, starts secretly with his friend, Candlewick, for the Land of Toys.

WHEN Pinocchio had calmed back to normal, the Fairy said to him: "Go if you like and invite your companions for the breakfast tomorrow, but remember to return home before dark. Have you understood?"

"I promise to be back in an hour," answered the puppet.

The puppet took leave of his good Fairy, who was like a mamma to him, and went out of the house singing and dancing.

In less than an hour all his friends were invited.

Now I must tell you that amongst Pinocchio's friends and school fellows he had a favourite, of whom he was very fond. This boy's name was Romeo; but he always went by the nickname of Candlewick, because he was so thin, straight, and bright – like the new wick of a little nightlight.

Candlewick was the laziest and the naughtiest boy in the school; but Pinocchio was devoted to him. In fact, Pinocchio had gone straight to his house to invite him to the breakfast – but he had not found Candlewick. He returned a second time, but Candlewick was not there. He went a third time, but it was in vain. Where could Pinocchio search for him? He looked here, there, and everywhere, and at last he saw him hiding in the porch of a farmer's cottage.

"What are you doing there?" asked Pinocchio, coming up to him.

"I am waiting for midnight, to set out..."

Pinocchio

"Why, where are you going?"

"Very far, very far, very far away."

"And I have been three times to your house to look for you."

"What did you want with me?"

"Do you not know the great event? Have you not heard of my good fortune?"

"What is it?"

"Tomorrow I cease to be a puppet, and I become a boy like you and like all the other boys."

"Well, good luck to you."

"So tomorrow I would like you to come to breakfast at my house."

"But I have just told you that I am going away tonight."

"And where are you going?"

"I am going to live in a country – the most delightful country in the world, a real land paradise!"

"What is it called?"

"It is called the Land of Toys. Why don't you come too?"

"I? No, never!"

"You are wrong, Pinocchio. Believe me, if you do not come you will wish you had. Where could you find a better country for us boys? There are no schools there; there are no teachers; there are no books. In that delightful land, nobody ever studies. On Thursdays there is no school – and every week consists of six Thursdays and one Sunday. Only think, the autumn holidays begin on the first of January and finish on the last day of December. That is the country for me! That is what all civilised countries should be like!"

"But how are the days spent in the Land of Toys?"

"They are spent in play and amusement from morning till night. When night comes you go to bed, and pick up the same life in the morning. What do you think of it?"

"Hmm..." said Pinocchio; and he shook his head slightly as much as to say, 'That is a life that I also would willingly lead.'

"Well, will you go with me? Yes or no? Make up your mind quickly."

"No, no, no, and again no. I promised my good Fairy to become a well-behaved boy, and I will keep my word. As I see that the sun is setting I must leave you at once and run away. Goodbye – and a pleasant journey to you."

"Where are you rushing off to in such a hurry?"

"Home. My good Fairy wishes me to be back before dark."

"Wait another two minutes."

"It will make me too late."

"Only two minutes."

"And if the Fairy scolds me?"

"Let her scold. When she has scolded well, she will hold her tongue," said that rascal Candlewick.

"And what are you going to do? Are you going alone or with companions?"

"Alone? There's going to be more than a hundred of us boys."

"And will you make the journey on foot?"

"A coach will pass by shortly which is going to take me to that happy country."

"What wouldn't I give for the coach to pass by now!"

"Why?"

"That I might see you all start together."

"Stay here a little longer and you will see us."

"No, no, I must go home."

"Wait another two minutes."

"I have already delayed too long. The Fairy will be anxious about me."

"Poor Fairy! Is she afraid that the bats will eat you?"

"But now," continued Pinocchio, "are you really certain that there are no schools in that country?"

"Not even the shadow of one."

"And no teachers either?..."

"Not one."

"And no one is ever made to study?"

"Never, never, never!"

"What a delightful country!" said Pinocchio, his mouth watering. "What a delightful country! I have never been there, but I can quite imagine it..."

"Why won't you come too?"

"It is useless to tempt me. I promised my good Fairy to become a sensible boy and I will not break my word."

"Goodbye, then, and give my compliments to all the boys of the schools, and also to those of the colleges, if you meet them in the street."

"Goodbye, Candlewick. A pleasant journey to you. Have fun – and think sometimes of your friends."

Thus saying, the puppet made two steps to go, but then stopped. Turning to his friend, he inquired: "But are you quite certain that in that country all the weeks consist of six Thursdays and one Sunday?"

"Most certain."

"But do you know for certain that the holidays begin on the first of January and finish on the last day of December?"

"Definitely."

"What a delightful country!" repeated Pinocchio, looking enchanted. Then with a determined air he added in a great hurry: "This time really goodbye, and a pleasant journey to you."

"Goodbye."

"When do you start, again?"

"Shortly."

"What a pity! If it was really only about an hour to the time of

your start, I should be almost tempted to wait."

"And the Fairy?"

"It is already late... If I return home an hour sooner or an hour later, it will be all the same."

"Poor Pinocchio! And if the Fairy scolds you?"

"I must put up with it! I will let her scold. When she has scolded well, she will hold her tongue."

In the meantime, night had come on and it was quite dark. Suddenly they saw in the distance a small light moving, and they heard a noise of talking, and the sound of a trumpet – but so small and feeble that it resembled the hum of a mosquito.

"Here it is!" shouted Candlewick, jumping to his feet.

"What is it?" asked Pinocchio in a whisper.

"It is the coach coming to take me. Now will you come, yes or no?"

Chapter 30

*Pinocchio goes to live in the Land of Toys,
and is happy there for five months...*

A T last the coach arrived; and it came without making the slightest noise, for its wheels were bound round with straw and rags.

It was drawn by twelve pairs of donkeys, all the same size but of different colours. Some were grey, some white, some brindled like pepper and salt, and others had large stripes of yellow and blue.

But the most extraordinary thing was this: the twelve pairs – that is the twenty-four donkeys – instead of being shod like other beasts of burden, had on their feet men's boots made of white kid.

And the coachman?

Picture to yourself a little man broader than he was long, flabby and greasy like a lump of butter, with a small round face like an orange, a little mouth that was always laughing, and a soft caressing voice like a cat when she is trying to coax herself into the good graces of the mistress of the house.

As soon as any boy saw the coachman he admired him, and boys always vied with each other in taking places in his coach to be conducted to the Land of Toys.

In fact, the coach was quite full of boys between eight and twelve years old, heaped one upon another like herrings in a barrel. They were uncomfortable, packed close together, and could hardly breathe. But nobody was complaining, nobody grumbling. The consolation of knowing that in a few hours they would reach a country where there were no books, no schools and no teachers had made them so happy and relaxed that they felt neither fatigue nor inconvenience, neither hunger, nor thirst, nor want of sleep.

As soon as the coach had drawn up, the little man turned to Candlewick and, with bows and smiles, said to him: "My dear child, there is not a place left in the coach. You can see for yourself that it is quite full..."

"No matter," replied Candlewick. "I will sit outside."

And giving a leap he seated himself astride one of the springs.

"And you, my dear!" said the little man, turning aimiably to Pinocchio.

"I am going home," answered Pinocchio. "I intend to study and to earn a good report at school, as all well-behaved boys do."

"May it bring you luck!"

"Pinocchio!" called out Candlewick. "Listen to me: come with us and we shall have such fun."

"No, no, no!"

"Come with us, and we shall have such fun," chorused a hundred voices from the inside of the coach.

"But if I come with you, what will my good Fairy say?" said the puppet, who was beginning to yield.

"Do not trouble your head with melancholy thoughts. Consider only that we are going to a country where we shall be at liberty to run riot from morning till night."

Pinocchio did not answer; but he sighed. He sighed again. He sighed for the third time, and he said finally: "Make a little room for me, for I am coming too."

"The places are all full," replied the little man. "But to show you how welcome you are, you shall have my seat outside on the driver's box."

Chapter 30

"And you?"

"Oh, I will go on foot."

"No, indeed, I could not allow that. I would rather mount one of these donkeys," cried Pinocchio.

He approached the right-hand donkey of the first pair and attempted to mount him, but the animal turned on him and, giving him a great blow in the stomach, rolled him over with his legs in the air.

You can imagine the raucous and riotous laughter of all the boys who witnessed this scene.

But the little man did not laugh. He approached the rebellious donkey and, pretending to give him a kiss, bit off half of his ear. He then said to the puppet: "Mount him now without fear. That little donkey had got some mischief into his head; but I whispered two little words into his ear which have, I hope, made him gentle and reasonable."

Pinocchio mounted and the coach started. Whilst the donkeys were galloping and the coach was rattling over the stones of the high road, the puppet thought that he heard a low voice that was scarcely intelligible saying to him: "Poor fool! You want to follow your own way, but you will be sorry!"

Pinocchio, feeling almost frightened, looked from side to side to try and discover where these words could come from: but he saw nobody. The donkeys galloped, the coach rattled, the boys inside slept, Candlewick snored like a dormouse, and the little man seated on the box sang between his teeth:

"During the night all sleep,
But I sleep never..."

After they had gone another mile, Pinocchio heard the same little low voice saying to him: "A day will come when you will weep as I am weeping now – but then it will be too late!"

Pinocchio

On hearing these words whispered very softly, the puppet, more frightened than ever, sprang down from the back of his donkey and went and took hold of his mouth.

Imagine his surprise when he found that the donkey was crying – and he was crying like a boy!

"Hey! Sir Coachman," cried Pinocchio to the little man. "Here is an extraordinary thing! This donkey is crying."

"Come, come," said the little man, "don't let us waste time in seeing a donkey cry. Mount him and let us go on: the night is cold and the road is long."

Pinocchio obeyed without another word.

In the morning about daybreak they arrived safely in the Land of Toys.

It was a country unlike any other country in the world. The population was composed entirely of boys. The oldest were fourteen and the youngest scarcely eight years old. In the streets there was such merriment, noise and shouting, that it was enough to turn anybody's head. There were troops of boys everywhere. Some were playing with marbles, some were playing racket games, some were playing with balls. Some rode bicycles, others wooden hobby horses. A party were playing at hide and seek; a few were chasing each other. Boys in scruffy clothes were eating treats; some were chanting, some singing, some leaping. To sum it all up, it was pandemonium. On the walls of the houses there were inscriptions written in charcoal: 'Long live playthings! We will have no more schools! Down with arithmetic!' and similar other fine sentiments – all in bad spelling.

Pinocchio, Candlewick, and the other boys who had made the journey with the little man had scarcely set foot in the town before they were in the thick of the tumult – and I need not tell you that in a few minutes they had made acquaintance with everybody. Where could happier or more contented boys be found?

Pinocchio

In the midst of continual games and every variety of amusement, the hours, the days, and the weeks passed like lightning.

Whenever Pinocchio by chance met Candlewick, the puppet remarked: "Oh, what a delightful life!"

"See, then, if I was not right?" replied the other. "And to think that you did not want to come! You must acknowledge that you owe this to me, to my advice and to my persuading. It is only friends who know how to do such good favours."

This delightful life went on for five months. The days were entirely spent in play and amusement, without a thought of books or school – until one morning Pinocchio awoke to a most disagreeable surprise that put him into a very bad humour.

Chapter 31

*Pinocchio gets donkey's ears – and then he
becomes a real little donkey and begins to bray.*

WHAT was this surprise?

I will tell you, my dear little readers. The surprise was that when Pinocchio awoke he scratched his head, and in scratching his head he discovered to his great astonishment that his ears had grown by more than a hand's length.

He went at once in search of a mirror so that he might look at himself, but not being able to find one he filled the basin of his washstand with water. There he saw reflected what he certainly never wanted to see. He saw his head embellished with a magnificent pair of donkey's ears!

Think of poor Pinocchio's sorrow, shame, and despair!

He began to cry and wail, and he beat his head against the wall. But the more he cried, the longer his ears grew. They grew, and grew, and became hairy towards the points.

At the sound of his loud outcries a beautiful little Marmot that lived on the first floor came into the room. Seeing the puppet in such grief she asked earnestly: "What has happened to you, my dear fellow-lodger?"

"I am ill, my dear little Marmot, very ill – and of an illness that frightens me. Do you understand counting a pulse?"

"A little."

"Then feel and see if by chance I have got a fever."

Pinocchio

The little Marmot raised her right forepaw and, after having felt Pinocchio's pulse, she said to him, sighing: "My friend, I am grieved to have to give you bad news!"

"What is it?"

"You have got a very bad fever!"

"What fever is it?"

"It is donkey fever," said the Marmot. "You must know that in two or three hours you will be no longer a puppet, or a boy. You will become really and truly a little donkey, like those that draw carts and carry cabbages and salad to market."

"Oh! How unlucky I am!" cried Pinocchio, seizing his two ears with his hands, and pulling them and tearing them furiously as if they had been someone else's ears.

"But is it really so?" asked the puppet, sobbing.

"It is indeed true!" said the Marmot. "All boys who are lazy, and who take a dislike to books, to schools and to teachers must end sooner or later by becoming transformed into so many little donkeys."

"But it was not my fault. Believe me, little Marmot, the fault was all Candlewick's! Ah! I should never have left that good Fairy who loved me like a mother and who had done so much for me! And I should be no longer a puppet – for I should by this time have become a little boy like so many others! But if I meet Candlewick, he'll be sorry! He shall hear what I think of him!"

And he turned to go out. But when he reached the door he remembered his donkey's ears and, feeling ashamed to show them in public, what do you think he did? He took a big cotton cap and, putting it on his head, he pulled it down over the point of his nose.

He then set out and went everywhere in search of Candlewick. He looked for him in the streets, in the squares, in the little theatres, in every possible place; but he could not find him. He inquired for him of everybody he met, but no one had seen him.

He then went to seek him at his house and, having reached the door, he knocked.

"Who is there?" asked Candlewick from within.

"It is I!" answered the puppet.

"Wait a moment and I will let you in."

After half an hour the door was opened – and imagine Pinocchio's feelings when, upon going into the room, he saw his friend Candlewick with a big cotton cap on his head which came down over his nose.

At the sight of the cap Pinocchio felt almost comforted and he thought to himself: 'Has my friend got the same illness that I have? Is he also suffering from donkey fever?' And pretending to have noticed nothing he asked him, smiling: "How are you, my dear Candlewick?"

"Very well; as well as a mouse in a Parmesan cheese."

"Are you saying that seriously?"

"Why should I tell you a lie?"

"Excuse me; but why, then, do you keep that cotton cap on your head which covers up your ears?"

"The doctor ordered me to wear it because I have hurt this knee. And you, dear puppet, why have you got on that cotton cap pulled down over your nose?"

"The doctor prescribed it because I have grazed my foot."

"Oh, poor Pinocchio!"

"Oh, poor Candlewick!"

After these words a long silence followed, during which the two friends did nothing but look mockingly at each other.

At last the puppet said in a soft, soothing voice to his companion: "Satisfy my curiosity, my dear Candlewick. Have you ever suffered from disease of the ears?"

"Never! And you?"

"Never! Only since this morning one of my ears aches."

Pinocchio

"Mine is also hurting me."

"You also? And which of your ears hurts you?"

"Both of them. And you?"

"Both of them. Can we have got the same illness?"

"I fear so."

"Will you do me a kindness, Candlewick?"

"Willingly! With all my heart."

"Will you let me see your ears?"

"Why not? But first, dear Pinocchio, I should like to see yours."

"No: you must be the first."

"No, friend! First you and then I!"

"Well," said the puppet, "let us come to an agreement like good friends."

"Let us hear it."

"We will both take off our caps at the same moment. Do you agree?"

"I agree."

"Then – attention!"

And Pinocchio began to count in a loud voice: "One! Two! Three!"

At the word 'Three!' the boys took off their caps and threw them into the air.

And then a scene followed that would sound incredible if it was not true. That is, that when Pinocchio and Candlewick discovered that they were both struck with the same misfortune, instead of feeling full of shame and grief, they began to prick up their ungainly ears and to make funny faces, and they ended by collapsing in gales of laughter.

Chapter 31

They laughed, and laughed, and laughed, until they had to hold themselves together. But in the midst of their merriment Candlewick suddenly stopped, staggered, and changing colour said to his friend: "Help, help, Pinocchio!"

"What is the matter with you?"

"Alas, I can no longer stand upright."

"No more can I," exclaimed Pinocchio, tottering and beginning to cry.

And whilst they were talking they both doubled up and began to run round the room on their hands and feet. And as they ran, their hands became hoofs, their faces lengthened into muzzles, and their backs became covered with a light grey hairy coat sprinkled with black.

But do you know what was the worst moment for these two wretched boys? The worst and the most humiliating moment was when their tails grew. Overcome by shame and sorrow they wept and bewailed their fate.

Oh, if they had but been wiser! But instead of sighs they could only bray like donkeys.

Whilst this was going on someone knocked at the door, and a voice on the outside said: "Open the door! I am the little man, I am the coachman, who brought you to this country. Open at once, or it will be the worse for you!"

Chapter 32

Pinocchio, having become a genuine little donkey, is taken to be sold, and is bought by the director of a circus troop to be taught to dance and to jump through hoops. But one evening the donkey becomes lame, and Pinocchio is then bought by a man who intends to make a drum out of his skin.

FINDING that the door remained shut, the little man burst it open with a violent kick. Coming into the room he said to Pinocchio and Candlewick with his usual little laugh: "Well done, boys! You brayed well, and I recognised you by your voices. That is why I am here."

At these words the two little donkeys were quite stupefied and stood with their heads down, their ears lowered, and their tails between their legs.

At first the little man took out a currycomb and groomed them well. When by this process he had polished them till they shone like two mirrors, he put a halter round their necks and led them to the marketplace, in the hope of selling them and making a good profit.

Indeed buyers were not wanting. Candlewick was bought by a farmer whose donkey had died the previous day. Pinocchio was sold to the director of a circus troop, who bought him intending to teach him to leap and to dance with the other animals belonging to the company.

From the very first day in the circus, Pinocchio had to endure a very hard, laborious life.

When he was put into his stall, his master filled the manger with straw; but Pinocchio, having tried a mouthful, spat it out again.

Chapter 32

Then his master, grumbling, filled the manger with hay – but neither did the hay please him.

"Ah!" exclaimed his master in a temper. "Does not hay please you either? Leave it to me, my fine donkey; if you are so full of fussiness I will find a way to cure you!" And by way of correcting him, he struck his legs with his whip.

Pinocchio began to cry and to bray with pain, and he said: "Eee-aw, eee-aw, I cannot digest straw!"

"Then eat hay!" said his master, who understood perfectly the donkey dialect.

"Eee-aw, eee-aw, hay gives me a pain in my stomach."

"Do you mean to pretend that a little donkey like you must be kept on breasts of chickens and the finest ducks?" asked his master, getting more and more angry, and whipping him again.

At this second whipping Pinocchio prudently held his tongue and said nothing more.

The stable was then shut and Pinocchio was left alone. He had not eaten for many hours and he began to yawn from hunger. Finding nothing else in the manger, he resigned himself and chewed a little hay; and after he had chewed it well, he shut his eyes and swallowed it.

"This hay is not bad," he said to himself, "but how much better it would have been if I had gone on with my studies! Instead of hay I might now be eating a hunk of new bread and a fine slice of sausage! But I must have patience!"

The next morning when he woke he looked in the manger for a little more hay; but he found none, for he had eaten it all during the night. Then he took a mouthful of chopped straw; but whilst he was chewing it he had to acknowledge that the taste of chopped straw did not in the least resemble a savoury dish of macaroni or rice.

"I must have patience!" he repeated as he went on chewing. "May my example serve at least as a warning to all disobedient boys who do not want to study!"

"Patience indeed!" shouted his master, coming at that moment into the stable. "Do you think, my little donkey, that I bought you only to give you food and drink? I bought you to make you work, that you might earn money for me. Up, then, at once! You must come with me into the circus, and there I will teach you to jump through hoops, to go through frames of paper headfirst, to dance waltzes and polkas, and to stand upright on your hind legs."

Poor Pinocchio, either by love or by force, had to learn all these fine things. But it took him three months before he had learnt them – and he got many a whipping that nearly took off his skin.

At last a day came when his master was able to announce that he would give a really extraordinary show. The many-coloured placards stuck on the street corners were thus worded:

GREATEST SHOW ON EARTH

TONIGHT
WILL TAKE PLACE THE USUAL FEATS
AND SURPRISING PERFORMANCES
EXECUTED BY ALL THE ARTISTES
AND BY ALL THE HORSES OF THE COMPANY,
AND MOREOVER
THE FAMOUS
LITTLE DONKEY PINOCCHIO,
CALLED
THE STAR OF THE DANCE,
WILL MAKE HIS FIRST APPEARANCE.

LIGHT SHOW IN THE THEATRE.

Chapter 32

On that evening, as you may imagine, an hour before the play was to begin the theatre was crammed. The benches round the circus were crowded with children and with boys of all ages, who were in a fever of impatience to see the famous little donkey Pinocchio dance.

When the first part of the performance was over, the director of the company, dressed in a black coat, white shorts, and big leather boots that came above his knees, presented himself to the public. After making a deep bow he began, very pompously, to make the following ridiculous speech: "Honoured guests, ladies and gentlemen! The humble undersigned being a passer-by in this illustrious city, I have wished to procure for myself the honour, not to say the pleasure, of presenting to his intelligent and distinguished audience a celebrated little donkey, who has already had the honour of dancing in the presence of His Majesty the Emperor of all the principal Courts of Europe. And thanking you, I beg of you to help us with your inspiring presence and to give us your kind attention."

This speech was received with much laughter and applause; but the applause doubled and became tumultuous when the little donkey Pinocchio made his appearance in the middle of the circus. He was decked out for the occasion. He had a new bridle of polished leather with brass buckles and studs, and two white camellia flowers in his ears. His mane was divided and curled, and each curl was tied with bows of coloured ribbon. He had a girth of gold and silver round his body, and his tail was plaited with amaranth and blue velvet ribbons. He was, in fact, a little donkey to fall in love with!

The director in presenting him to the public added these few words: "My honoured audience! I am not here to tell you falsehoods of the great difficulties that I have overcome in understanding and taming this beast, whilst he was grazing at liberty amongst the mountains on the plains in the wilderness. I beg you will observe the wild rolling of his eyes! I tried every means to tame him and to accustom him to the life of domestic animals – but in vain, until I was often forced to use the convincing argument of the whip. But all my goodness to him, instead of gaining his affections, has, on the contrary, increased his viciousness. However, following a French method, I discovered on his skull a bony bump, that the Faculty of Medicine in Paris has itself recognised as the root of his talent for being as nimble on his feet as a human. For this reason I have not only taught him to dance, but also to jump through hoops and through frames covered with paper. Admire him and see for yourselves! But before I take my leave of you, permit me, ladies and gentlemen, to invite you to the daily performance that will take place tomorrow evening. However, in the event that the weather should threaten rain, the performance will be postponed till tomorrow morning at eleven o'clock."

Here the director made another deep bow. Then turning to Pinocchio he said: "Courage, Pinocchio! Before you begin your feats make your bow to this distinguished audience: ladies, gentlemen, and children."

Pinocchio obeyed and bent both his knees till they touched the ground. He remained kneeling until the director, cracking his whip, shouted to him: "March!"

Then the little donkey raised himself on his four legs and began to walk round the theatre, keeping to a marching pace.

After a little the director cried: "Trot!" and Pinocchio, obeying the order, changed to a trot.

"Canter!" and Pinocchio broke into a canter.

"Full gallop!" and Pinocchio went full gallop. But whilst he was going full speed like a racehorse the director, raising his arm in the air, fired off a pistol. At the shot, the little donkey, pretending to be wounded, fell headlong in the circus ring, as if he was really dying.

Then, as he got up from the ground amidst an outburst of applause, shouts, and clapping of hands, he naturally raised his head

and looked up – and he saw in one of the boxes a beautiful lady who wore round her neck a thick gold chain from which hung a medallion. On the medallion was painted the portrait of a puppet.

"That is my portrait! That lady is the Fairy!" said Pinocchio to himself, recognising her immediately. Overcome with delight he tried to cry: "Oh, my little Fairy! Oh, my little Fairy!" But instead of these words a bray came from his throat, so loud and long that all the spectators laughed – especially all the children who were in the theatre.

Then the director, to give him a lesson, and to make him understand that it is not good manners to bray before the public, gave him a blow on his nose with the handle of his whip.

The poor little donkey put his tongue out an inch, and licked his nose for at least five minutes, thinking perhaps that it would ease the pain he felt. But imagine his despair when, looking up a second time, he saw that the box was empty and that the Fairy had disappeared!

He thought he was going to die. His eyes filled with tears and he began to weep. Nobody, however, noticed it – least of all the director who, cracking his whip, shouted: "Courage, Pinocchio! Now let the audience see how gracefully you can jump through the hoops."

Pinocchio tried two or three times, but each time that he came in front of the hoop, instead of going through it, he found it easier to go under it. At last he made a leap and went through it; but his right leg unfortunately caught in the hoop, and that caused him to fall to the ground doubled up in a heap on the other side.

When he got up, he found he was lame! It was only with great difficulty that he managed to return to the stable.

"Bring out Pinocchio! We want the little donkey! Bring out the little donkey!" shouted all the boys in the theatre, touched and sorry for the sad accident.

But the little donkey was seen no more that evening.

Chapter 32

The following morning, the vet – that is, animal doctor – paid him a visit and declared that he would remain lame for life.

The circus director then said to the stable-boy: "What do you think I can do with a lame donkey? He would eat food without earning it. Take him to the market and sell him."

The stable-boy took Pinocchio to the market, where a purchaser was found at once. He asked the stable-boy: "How much do you want for that lame donkey?"

"Twenty francs."

"I will give you twenty pence. Don't suppose that I am buying him to make use of; I am buying him solely for his skin. I see that his skin is very hard, and I intend to make a drum with it for the band of my village."

I shall leave it to you, my readers, to imagine poor Pinocchio's feelings when he heard that he was destined to become a drum!

As soon as the buyer had paid his twenty pence he conducted the little donkey to the seashore. He then put a stone round his neck and, tying a rope around his leg, while holding the other end in his hand, he gave him a sudden push and threw him into the water.

Pinocchio, weighed down by the stone, went at once to the bottom. His owner, keeping tight hold of the cord, sat down quietly on a piece of rock to wait until the little donkey was drowned, intending then to skin him.

Chapter 33

Pinocchio, having been thrown into the sea, is eaten by the fish and becomes a puppet as he was before. Whilst he is swimming away to save his life he is swallowed by the terrible Dogfish shark.

AFTER Pinocchio had been fifty minutes under the water, his purchaser said aloud to himself:

"My poor little lame donkey must by this time be quite drowned. I will therefore pull him out of the water and I will make a fine drum of his skin."

And he began to haul in the rope that he had tied to the donkey's leg. He hauled, and hauled, and hauled, until at last – what do you think appeared above the water? Instead of a little dead donkey he saw a live puppet, who was wriggling like an eel.

Seeing this wooden puppet the poor man thought he was dreaming. Struck dumb with astonishment he remained with his mouth open and his eyes popping out of his head.

Having somewhat recovered from his first amazement, he asked in a quavering voice: "And the little donkey that I threw into the sea? What has become of him?"

"I am the little donkey!" said Pinocchio, laughing.

"You?"

"I."

"Ah, you young scamp! Do you dare to make fun of me? How can you, who but a short time ago were a little donkey, have become a wooden puppet, only from having been left in the water?"

Chapter 33

"It must have been the effect of seawater. The sea makes extraordinary changes."

"Beware, puppet! You will be sorry, if I lose patience!"

"Well, master, do you wish to know the true story? If you will set my leg free I will tell it to you."

The good man, who was curious to hear the true story, immediately untied the knot that kept the puppet bound. Pinocchio, finding himself as free as a bird in the air, made a spring and plunged into the water. Swimming gaily away from the shore he called to his poor owner: "Goodbye, master; if you should be in want of a skin to make a drum, remember me."

And he laughed and went on swimming. In the twinkling of an eye he had swum so far off that he was scarcely visible. All that could be seen of him was a little black speck on the surface of the sea that from time to time lifted its legs out of the water and leapt and capered like a dolphin enjoying himself.

Whilst Pinocchio was swimming, he saw in the midst of the sea a rock that seemed to be made of white marble. On the summit there stood a beautiful little goat who bleated lovingly and made signs to him to approach. But the most singular thing was this. The little goat's hair, instead of being white or black – or a mixture of two colours as is usual with other goats – was blue... and of a very vivid blue, greatly resembling the hair of the beautiful child.

I leave you to imagine how rapidly poor Pinocchio's heart began to beat. He swam with redoubled strength and energy towards the white rock... He was already halfway when he saw, rising up out of the water and coming to meet him, the horrible head of a sea-monster! His wide-open cavernous mouth and his three rows of enormous teeth would have been terrifying to look at even in a picture.

And do you know what this sea-monster was?

This sea-monster was neither more nor less than that gigantic

Pinocchio

Dogfish shark who has been mentioned many times in this story, and who for his slaughter and for his insatiable cruelty had been named 'the Attila of the Ocean'!

Only think of poor Pinocchio's terror at the sight of the monster. He tried to avoid it, to change his direction. He tried to escape; but that immense wide-open mouth came towards him with the swiftness of an arrow.

"Be quick, Pinocchio, for pity's sake," cried the beautiful little goat.

And Pinocchio swam desperately with his arms, his chest, his legs, and his feet.

"Quick, Pinocchio, the monster is close upon you!"

And Pinocchio swam quicker than ever, and flew on with the speed of a bullet from a gun. He had nearly reached the rock. The little goat leant over towards the sea and stretched out her forelegs to help him out of the water! But it was too late!

Chapter 33

The monster overtook him! And, drawing in his breath, he sucked in the poor puppet as he would have sucked a hen's egg. He swallowed him with such a greedy gulp that Pinocchio received such a blow when he fell into the Dogfish's stomach that he remained unconscious for a quarter of an hour afterwards.

When he came to again after the shock, he could not imagine where he was. All round him it was quite dark. The darkness was so black and so deep that it seemed to him that he had fallen headfirst into an inkstand full of ink. He listened but he could hear no noise; only from time to time great gusts of wind blew in his face. At first he could not understand where the wind came from, but at last he discovered that it came out of the monster's lungs. For you must know that the Dogfish shark suffered very much from asthma, and when he breathed it was exactly as if a north wind was blowing.

Pinocchio at first tried to keep up his courage; but when he had one proof after another that he was really shut up in the body of this sea-monster, he began to cry and scream and to sob out: "Help! Help! Oh, how unfortunate I am! Will nobody come to save me?"

"Who do you think could save you, you miserable wretch?" said a voice in the dark that sounded like a guitar out of tune.

"Who is speaking?" asked Pinocchio, frozen with terror.

"It is I! I am a poor Tunny who was swallowed by the Dogfish at the same time that you were. And what fish are you?"

"I have nothing in common with fish. I am a puppet."

"Then if you are not a fish, why did you let yourself be swallowed by the monster?"

"I didn't let myself be swallowed: the monster just swallowed me! And now what are we to do here in the dark?"

"Resign ourselves to our fate and wait until the Dogfish has digested us both."

"But I do not want to be digested!" howled Pinocchio, crying again.

"Neither do I want to be digested," added the Tunny. "But I am enough of a philosopher to comfort myself by thinking that when one is born a Tunny it is more dignified to die in the water than in oil."

"That is all nonsense!" cried Pinocchio.

"It is my opinion," replied the Tunny, "and opinions, so say the political Tunnies, ought to be respected."

"To sum it all up – I want to get away from here, I want to escape."

"Escape if you are able!"

"Is this Dogfish who has swallowed us very big?" asked the puppet.

"Big! Why, imagine, his body is two miles long – without counting his tail."

Whilst they were holding this conversation in the dark, Pinocchio thought that he saw a light a long way off.

"What is that little light I see in the distance?" he asked.

"It is most likely some companion in misfortune who is waiting, like us, to be digested."

"I will go and find him. Do you not think that it may by chance be some old fish who perhaps could show us how to escape?"

"I hope it may be so with all my heart, dear puppet."

"Goodbye, Tunny."

"Goodbye, puppet, and good luck to you."

"Shall we meet again?"

"Who can say? It is better not even to think of it!"

Chapter 34

Pinocchio finds in the body of the Dogfish shark – whom does he find? Read this chapter and you will know.

PINOCCHIO, having taken leave of his friend the Tunny, began to grope his way in the dark through the body of the Dogfish, taking a step at a time in the direction of the light that he saw shining dimly at a great distance.

The farther he advanced, the brighter became the light. He walked and walked until at last he reached it. And when he reached it – what did he find? I will give you a thousand guesses. He found a little table spread out, and on it a lighted candle stuck into a green glass bottle, and seated at the table was a little old man. He was eating some live fish, and they were so very much alive that whilst he was eating them they sometimes even jumped out of his mouth.

At this sight Pinocchio was filled with such great and unexpected joy that he was beside himself. He wanted to laugh, he wanted to cry, he wanted to say a thousand things, but instead he could only stammer out a few confused and broken words. At last he succeeded in uttering a cry of joy and, opening his arms, he threw them round the little old man's neck, and began to shout: "Oh, my dear papa! I have found you at last! I will never leave you again, never again, never again!"

"Can I really believe my eyes?" said the little old man, rubbing his eyes. "Are you really my dear Pinocchio?"

"Yes, yes, I am Pinocchio – really Pinocchio! And you have quite forgiven me, have you not? Oh, my dear papa, how good you are! And to think that I, on the contrary... Oh! But if you only knew what misfortunes have been poured on my head, and all that has befallen me! Only imagine, the day that you, poor dear Papa, sold your coat to buy me an ABC book that I might go to school, I escaped to see the puppet show. The showman wanted to put me on the fire so that I might roast his mutton – and he was the same that afterwards gave me five gold pieces to take them to you. But I met the Fox and the Cat, who took me to the inn of the Red Lobster, where they ate like wolves. And I left by myself in the middle of the night, and I encountered outlaws who ran after me, and I ran away, and they followed, and I ran, and they always followed me, and I ran, until they hung me to a branch of a Big Oak. And the beautiful child with blue hair sent a little carriage to fetch me, and the doctors when they had seen me said immediately, 'If he is not dead, it is a proof that he is still alive'. And then by chance I told a lie and my nose began to grow until I could no longer get through the door of the room, for which reason I went with the Fox and the Cat to bury the four gold pieces – for one I had spent at the inn – and the Parrot began to laugh... and instead of two thousand gold pieces I found none left. For which reason the judge, when he heard that I had been robbed, had me immediately put in prison to content the robbers. And then when I was coming away I saw a beautiful bunch of grapes in a field, and I was caught in a trap, and the farmer, who was quite right, put a dog collar round my neck so that I might guard the poultry-yard, and acknowledging my innocence he let me go. And the Serpent with the smoking tail began to laugh and burst a blood-vessel in his chest. And so I returned to the house of the beautiful child – who was dead... and the Pigeon, seeing that I was crying, said to me, 'I have seen your father, who was building a little boat to go in search of you,' and I said to him, 'Oh! If I had also wings,' and he said to me, 'Do you want to go to your father?' and I said, 'Without doubt! But who will take me to him?' and he said to me, 'I will take you,' and I said to him 'How?' and he said to me, 'Get on my back,' and so we flew all night, and then in the morning all the fishermen who were looking out to sea said to me, 'There is a poor man in a boat who is on the point of being drowned,' and I recognised you at once, even at that distance, for my heart told me, and I made signs to you to return to land..."

"I also recognised you," said Geppetto, "and I would willingly have returned to the shore. But what was I to do? The sea was tremendous and a great wave upset my boat. Then a horrible Dogfish shark who was near saw me in the water and came straight towards me and, putting out his tongue, took hold of me and swallowed me as if I had been a little Bologna tart."

"And how long have you been shut up here?" asked Pinocchio.

"Since that day – it must be nearly two years ago. Two years, my dear Pinocchio, that have seemed to me like two centuries!"

"And how have you managed to live? And where did you get the candle? And the matches to light it? Who gave them to you?"

"Stop, and I will tell you everything. Know, then, that in the same storm in which my boat was upset a merchant vessel foundered. The sailors were all saved but the vessel went to the bottom, and the Dogfish, who had that day an excellent appetite, after he had swallowed me, swallowed also the merchant vessel."

"How?"

"He swallowed it in one mouthful, and the only thing that he spat out was the main mast, that had stuck between his teeth like a fishbone. Fortunately for me the vessel was laden with preserved meat in tins, biscuits, bottles of wine, dried raisins, cheese, coffee, sugar, candles, and boxes of matches. With this fortunate supply I have been able to live for two years. But I have arrived at the end of my resources: there is nothing left in the larder – and this candle that you see burning is the only one that remains."

"And after that?"

"After that, dear boy, we shall both remain in the dark."

"Then, dear little Papa," said Pinocchio, "there is no time to lose. We must think of escaping."

"Of escaping? How?"

"We must escape through the mouth of the Dogfish, throw ourselves into the sea and swim away."

"You talk well: but, dear Pinocchio, I don't know how to swim."

"What does that matter? I am a good swimmer, and you can get on my shoulders and I will carry you safely to shore."

"All dreams, my boy!" replied Geppetto, shaking his head with a melancholy smile. "Do you suppose it possible that a puppet like you, scarcely a metre high, could have the strength to swim with me on his shoulders?"

"Try it and you will see!"

Without another word, Pinocchio took the candle in his hand and, going in front to light the way, he said to his father: "Follow me, and don't be afraid."

They walked for some time and traversed the body and the stomach of the Dogfish shark. But when they had arrived at the point where the monster's big throat began, they thought it better to stop to have a good look round and to choose the best moment for escaping.

Now I must tell you that the Dogfish, being very old, and suffering from asthma and heart palpitations was obliged to sleep with his mouth open. Pinocchio, therefore, having approached the entrance to his throat and looking up, could see beyond the enormous gaping mouth a large piece of starry sky and beautiful moonlight.

"This is the moment to escape," he whispered to his father. "The Dogfish is sleeping like a dormouse, the sea is calm, and it is as light as day. Follow me, dear Papa, and in a short time we shall be safe."

Pinocchio

They immediately climbed up the throat of the sea-monster and, having reached his immense mouth, they began to walk on tiptoe down his tongue.

Before taking the final leap the puppet said to his father: "Get on my shoulders and put your arms tight round my neck. I will take care of the rest."

As soon as Geppetto was firmly settled on his son's shoulders, Pinocchio, feeling sure of himself, threw himself into the water and began to swim. The sea was as smooth as oil, the moon shone brilliantly, and the Dogfish was sleeping so profoundly that even cannon fire would have failed to wake him.

Chapter 35

Pinocchio at last ceases to be a puppet and becomes a boy.

WHILST Pinocchio was swimming quickly towards the shore he discovered that his father, who was on his shoulders with his legs in the water, was trembling as violently as if the poor man had a high fever.

Was he trembling from cold or from fear? Perhaps a little from both the one and the other. But Pinocchio, thinking that it was from fear, said to comfort him: "Courage, Papa! In a few minutes we shall be safely on shore."

"But where is this blessed shore?" asked the little old man, becoming still more frightened, and screwing up his eyes as tailors do when they wish to thread a needle. "I have been looking in every direction and I see nothing except the sky and the sea."

"But I see the shore as well," said the puppet. "You must know that I am like a cat: I see better by night than by day."

Poor Pinocchio was making a pretence of being in good spirits, but in reality... in reality he was beginning to feel discouraged – his strength was failing, he was gasping and panting for breath. He could do no more, and the shore was still far off.

He swam until he had no breath left; then he turned his head to Geppetto and said in broken gasps: "Papa... help me... I am dying!"

The father and son were on the point of drowning when they heard a voice like a guitar out of tune saying: "Who is it that is dying?"

"It is I, and my poor father!"

Pinocchio

"I know that voice! You are Pinocchio!"

"Precisely: and you?"

"I am the Tunny, your prison companion in the body of the Dogfish shark."

"And how did you manage to escape?"

"I followed your example. You showed me the road and I escaped after you."

"Tunny, you have arrived at the right moment! I implore you to help us, or we are lost."

"Willingly and with all my heart. You must both of you take hold of my tail and leave me to guide you. I will take you on shore in four minutes."

Geppetto and Pinocchio, I need not tell you, accepted the offer at once. However, instead of holding on by his tail they thought it would be more comfortable to get on the Tunny's back.

Having reached the shore, Pinocchio sprang first on land that he might help his father to do the same. He then turned to the Tunny and said to him in a voice full of emotion: "My friend, you have saved my papa's life. I can find no words with which to thank you properly. Allow me at least to give you a kiss as a sign of my eternal gratitude!"

The Tunny put his head out of the water and Pinocchio, kneeling on the ground, kissed him tenderly on his face. At this spontaneous proof of warm affection the poor Tunny, who was not accustomed to it, felt extremely touched. Ashamed to let himself be seen crying like a child he plunged under the water and disappeared.

By this time the day had dawned. Pinocchio then offered his arm to Geppetto, who had scarcely breath to stand, and said to him: "Lean on my arm, dear Papa, and let us go. We will walk very slowly, and when we are tired we can rest by the wayside."

"And where shall we go?" asked Geppetto.

"In search of some house or cottage, where they will give us for charity a mouthful of bread and a little straw to serve as a bed."

They had not gone a hundred yards when they saw by the roadside two villainous-looking individuals begging.

They were the Cat and the Fox, but they were scarcely recognisable. Fancy! The Cat had so long feigned blindness that she had become blind in reality; and the Fox, old, mangy, and with one side paralysed, had not even his tail left. That sneaking thief, having fallen into the most squalid misery, one fine day had found himself obliged to sell his beautiful tail to a travelling pedlar, who bought it to drive away flies.

"Oh, Pinocchio!" cried the Fox. "Give a little in charity to two poor, infirm people."

"Infirm people," repeated the Cat.

"Begone, tricksters!" answered the puppet. "You took me in once, but you will never catch me again."

"Believe me, Pinocchio, we are now poor and unfortunate indeed!"

"If you are poor, you deserve it. Remember the proverb: 'Stolen money never brings happiness'. Begone, tricksters!"

And thus saying Pinocchio and Geppetto went their way in peace. When they had gone another hundred yards they saw, at the end of a path in the middle of the fields, a nice little straw hut with a roof of tiles and bricks.

"That hut must be inhabited by someone," said Pinocchio. "Let us go and knock at the door." So they went and knocked.

"Who is there?" said a little voice from within.

"We are a poor father and son without bread and without a roof," answered the puppet.

"Turn the key and the door will open," said the same little voice.

Pinocchio turned the key and the door opened. They went in and looked here, there, and everywhere, but could see no one.

"Oh! Where is the master of the house?" said Pinocchio, much surprised.

"Here! I am up here!"

The father and son looked immediately up to the ceiling and there on a beam they saw the Talking Cricket.

"Oh, my dear little Cricket!" said Pinocchio, bowing politely to him.

"Ah! Now you call me 'your dear little Cricket'. But do you remember the time when you threw a hammer at me, to drive me from your house?"

"You are right, Cricket! Drive me away also. Throw a hammer at me – but have pity on my poor papa."

"I will have pity on both father and son; I just wished to remind you of the ill treatment I received from you, to teach you that in this world, we should show courtesy to everybody, whenever possible, if we wish it to be extended to us in our hour of need."

"You are right, Cricket, you are right, and I will bear in mind the lesson you have given me. But tell me how you managed to buy this beautiful hut."

"This hut was given to me yesterday by a goat whose wool was of a beautiful blue colour."

"And where has the goat gone?" asked Pinocchio, very curious.

"I do not know."

"And when will it come back?"

"It will never come back. It went away yesterday in great grief. It seemed to be bleating: 'Poor Pinocchio! I shall never see him again. For by this time the Dogfish shark must have devoured him!'"

"Did it really say that? Then it was she! It was she! It was my dear little Fairy!" exclaimed Pinocchio, crying and sobbing.

When he had cried for some time he dried his eyes and prepared a comfortable bed of straw for Geppetto to lie down upon. Then he asked the Cricket: "Tell me, little Cricket, where can I find a tumbler of milk for my poor papa?"

"Three fields off from here there lives a gardener called Giangio who keeps cows. Go to him and you will get the milk you want."

Pinocchio ran all the way to Giangio's house. There the gardener asked him: "How much milk do you want?"

"I want a tumblerful."

"A tumbler of milk costs a halfpenny. Begin by giving me the halfpenny."

"I have not even a farthing," replied Pinocchio, dismayed and ashamed.

"That is bad, puppet," answered the gardener. "If you have not even a farthing, I have not even a drop of milk."

"I will just have to be patient then!" said Pinocchio, and he turned to go.

"Wait a little," said Giangio. "We can come to an arrangement together. Will you undertake to turn the pumping machine?"

"What is the pumping machine?"

"It is a wooden pole which serves to draw up the water from the well to water the vegetables."

"I will try."

"Well, then, if you will draw a hundred buckets of water, I will give you in compensation a tumbler of milk."

"It is a bargain."

Giangio then led Pinocchio to the kitchen garden and taught him how to turn the pumping machine. Pinocchio immediately began to work; but before he had drawn up the hundred buckets of water the perspiration was pouring from his head to his feet. Never before had he felt so exhausted.

"Up till now," said the gardener, "the work of turning the pumping machine was performed by my little donkey; but the poor animal is dying."

"Will you take me to see him?" said Pinocchio.

"Willingly."

Pinocchio

When Pinocchio went into the stable, he saw a beautiful little donkey stretched on the straw, worn out from hunger and overwork. After looking at him earnestly he said to himself, much troubled: "I am sure I know this little donkey! His face is not new to me." And bending over him he asked him in donkey language: "Who are you?"

At this question the little donkey opened his dying eyes and answered in broken words in the same language: "I am...Can...dle... wick..." And having again closed his eyes, he expired.

"Oh, poor Candlewick!" said Pinocchio in a low voice, and took a handful of straw to dry a tear that was rolling down his face.

"Do you grieve for a donkey that cost you nothing?" said the gardener. "Imagine what it is like for me, who bought him for ready money?"

"I must tell you – he was my friend!"

"Your friend?"

"One of my school fellows!"

"What?" shouted Giangio, laughing loudly. "How? You had donkeys for school fellows? I can imagine what wonderful lessons you must have had!"

The puppet, who felt much embarrassed at these words, did not answer; but taking his tumbler of milk, still quite warm, he returned to the hut.

And from that day for more than five months Pinocchio continued to get up at daybreak every morning to go and turn the pumping machine, to earn the tumbler of milk that was of such benefit to his father in his bad state of health. But this was not enough for him; for in his spare time he learnt to make hampers and baskets of rushes, and with the money he obtained from selling them he was able to provide for all the daily expenses, being very careful with his pennies. He constructed, amongst other things an elegant little wheelchair in which he could take his father out on fine days to breathe some fresh air.

By his hard work, creativity and eagerness to work and to overcome difficulties, Pinocchio not only succeeded in supporting his sick father in comfort, but he also managed to put aside forty pence to buy himself a new coat.

One morning he said to his father: "I am going to the neighbouring market to buy myself a jacket, a cap, and a pair of shoes. When I return," he added, laughing, "I shall be so well dressed that you will take me for a fine gentleman."

Leaving the house he began to run merrily and happily along. All at once he heard himself called by name and, turning round, he saw a big Snail crawling out from the hedge.

"Do you not know me?" asked the Snail.

"It seems to me... and yet I am not sure..."

"Do you not remember the Snail who was maid to the Fairy with blue hair? Do you not remember the time when I came downstairs to let you in and you were caught by your foot, which you had stuck through the house door?"

"I remember it all," cried Pinocchio. "Tell me quickly, my beautiful little Snail, where have you left my good Fairy? What is she doing? Has she forgiven me? Does she still remember me? Does she still wish me well? Is she far from here? Can I go and see her?"

To all these rapid breathless questions the Snail replied in her usual unruffled manner: "My dear Pinocchio, the poor Fairy is lying in bed at the hospital!"

"At the hospital?"

"Indeed, it is true. Overtaken by a thousand misfortunes, she has fallen seriously ill; she has not even enough to buy herself a mouthful of bread."

"Is it really so? Oh, how sorrowful you have made me! Oh, poor Fairy! Poor Fairy! Poor Fairy! If I had a million I would run and carry it to her, but I have only forty pence – here they are. I was going to buy a new coat. Take them, Snail, and carry them at once to my good Fairy."

"And your new coat?"

"What does my new coat matter? I would sell even these rags that I have got on to be able to help her. Go, Snail, and be quick. In two days return to this place, for I hope I shall then be able to give you some more money. Up to this time I have worked to support my papa: from today I will work five hours more so that I may also support my good mamma. Goodbye, Snail, I shall expect you in two days."

The Snail, contrary to her usual habits, began to run like a lizard in a hot August sun.

That evening Pinocchio, instead of going to bed at ten o'clock, sat up till midnight had struck; and instead of making eight baskets of rushes he made sixteen. Then he went to bed and fell asleep. And whilst he slept he thought that he saw the Fairy, smiling and beautiful, who, after having kissed him said to him: "Well done, Pinocchio! To reward you for your good heart I will forgive you for all that is past. Boys who look after their parents tenderly and help them in old age and sickness are deserving of great praise and love, even if they cannot be held up as models of obedience and good behaviour. Try and do better in the future and you will be happy."

At this moment his dream ended, and Pinocchio opened his eyes and awoke.

Imagine his astonishment when, upon awakening, he discovered that he was no longer a wooden puppet, but that he had become instead a boy, like all other boys! He gave a glance round and saw that the straw walls of the hut had disappeared and that he was in a pretty little room furnished and arranged with a simplicity that was almost elegance. Jumping out of bed, he found a new suit of clothes ready for him, a new cap, and a pair of new leather boots.

Pinocchio was hardly dressed when he naturally put his hands in his pockets – and pulled out a little ivory purse on which these words were written: 'The Fairy with blue hair returns the forty pence to her dear Pinocchio and thanks him for his good heart'. He opened the purse and instead of forty copper pennies he saw forty shining gold pieces fresh from the mint.

He then went and looked at himself in the glass – and he thought he was someone else. For he no longer saw the usual reflection of a wooden puppet; he was greeted instead by the image of a bright, intelligent boy with chestnut hair and blue eyes – and looking as happy and joyful as if it were the Easter holidays.

In the midst of all these wonders, one after the other, Pinocchio felt quite bewildered. He could not tell if he was really awake or if he was dreaming with his eyes open.

"Where can my papa be?" he exclaimed suddenly. Going into the next room he found old Geppetto quite well, lively, and in good humour, just as he had been formerly. He had already resumed his trade of wood carving, and he was designing a rich and beautiful frame of leaves, flowers, and the heads of animals.

"Satisfy my curiosity, dear Papa," said Pinocchio, throwing his arms round his neck and covering him with kisses. "How can this sudden change be accounted for?"

"This sudden change in our home is all your doing," answered Geppetto.

"How my doing?"

"Because when boys who have behaved badly turn over a new leaf and become good, they have the power of bringing content and happiness to their families."

"And where has the old wooden Pinocchio hidden himself?"

"There he is," answered Geppetto, and he pointed to a big puppet leaning against a chair, with its head on one side, its arms dangling,

Pinocchio

and its legs so crossed and bent that it was really a miracle that it remained standing.

Pinocchio turned and looked at it, and after he had looked at it for a short time, he said to himself with great content: "How ridiculous I was when I was a puppet! And how happy I am, now that I have become a real little boy!"